Birthday Surprise

A Legacy Series Reunion, Book 2

PAULA KAY

ISBN: 0976551624
ISBN-13: 978-0976551621

DEDICATION

To my readers,
for loving these characters as much as I do.

TABLE OF CONTENTS

CHAPTER 1

Gigi grinned for the photo at Douglas's request, laughing when instead of smiling, he surprised her with a kiss just as he snapped the picture.

"Look, honey, it's the perfect photo of us with the Eiffel Tower in the background."

Gigi took the phone from him to get a closer look. "Well, you've certainly become quite the expert at taking selfies of us, haven't you?" She laughed, handed him the phone, and took his hand to pull him in close to her. "And I don't think I've thanked you near enough for this incredible trip, my darling."

Douglas kissed her. "I've never loved Paris as much as when I've been here with you. Somehow you just make everything that much more exciting and beautiful."

Gigi laughed. "Could it be the fact that I'm your perfect partner in crime when it comes to eating all the crepes in the entire city?"

They'd been to Paris a few times together, but in all their eighteen years of marriage they'd not ever had a trip as romantic as the past week had been. And Gigi knew how lucky they were.

Douglas laughed too. "Speaking of crepes…"

Gigi laughed. "Sure, let's stop at our favorite place on the way back. I could use a little something sweet."

He kissed her and grabbed her hand. They walked in easy silence for a few minutes, enjoying the sights and sounds around them. What was said about April in Paris was true. It seemed magical to Gigi and she wasn't sure if she was ready for it to end—a bit of a surprise to her, because she was almost always missing their home back in Tuscany whenever they were away.

And she had the party to look forward to. The thought reminded her that she owed Lia a phone call. She checked her phone to reread the last text to her.

"Everything okay?"

"Yeah, I just forgot to call Lia back earlier. I guess I should wait until morning."

"Party planning?"

"Kind of." Gigi laughed lightly. "I must say, I'm quite in the dark about this party—not that I don't think Lia has it all planned and it will be beautiful, but she's definitely being very tight-lipped about it all."

"Well, darling. Maybe they want to surprise you—with some things, I mean."

"Because I love surprises so much?"

"You do love surprises, don't you?"

He was teasing her. She loved it when Douglas

surprised her, which was actually quite often.

She leaned over to kiss him on the cheek. "Yes, I do like surprises, I suppose—the good kind, that is."

"Of course—only good surprises for you." Douglas stopped to check his own phone.

"Is something wrong?"

Gigi could always tell when he got a text or email that needed attention. He'd been officially retired for years now, but he still did some consulting and had his hands in a few things back in San Francisco that still needed his attention.

He looked up from his phone. "Oh, no. Nothing's wrong. I just need to make a few calls when we get back to the apartment—after our dessert."

They only had to walk a short distance to the apartment that Douglas had rented for them. It had a balcony and the most perfect view of the Eiffel Tower. The past mornings had been spent sitting together on their balcony, drinking coffee and eating the most exquisite croissants from the nearby bakery. Gigi wasn't at all sure she was ready to leave in just two days.

"So, what's on your agenda for our remaining days?"

"Who has an agenda around here?" She grinned at him. They traveled well together, both content to not over-plan and to let the days unfold as they did. "Well, I do have that lunch date with Blu for the day after tomorrow. Are you sure you don't want to join us? You're welcome to."

Douglas shook his head. "No, no. You two have your time together. I've got a little bit of work to do anyway, so I'll do it then. How long is she in town for?"

"Just the one night, I think. We've never been in Paris at the same time, so we might also do a bit of shopping."

Douglas laughed. "I knew there would be shopping!"

Gigi laughed too. She rarely shopped for herself, and usually her shopping did involve the expert eye of Blu. It certainly helped to have a fashion designer for a friend, that was for sure.

"Oh, she just has this one shop she wants to take me to. Maybe I'll buy something new for the party."

"That sounds like a lovely idea. Of course you should get yourself a new dress."

They stopped on the corner with their favorite place to buy sweet crepes.

"Chocolate?"

"You know me so well. And promise me you're going to support me going on a diet when we get back." She laughed, but she really could feel that she'd put on a few pounds since they'd been away.

Douglas grabbed her around the waist and kissed her squarely on the mouth. "Nonsense. You're absolutely gorgeous, woman—every inch of you. And of course I'll support you, darling, with whatever you need."

"Well, right now, I need you to hand me a napkin, please, before this chocolate drips all down the front of me." Gigi laughed and followed Douglas to a nearby bench where they sat finishing their desserts.

It was hard to believe that she was turning seventy next week. She certainly didn't feel like a seventy-year-old woman—whatever that was supposed to feel like—and whenever she and Douglas were together, half the time she thought they acted like a couple of teenagers in love.

He grabbed her hand and then rubbed his finger lightly near her mouth, bringing it away with just a dash of chocolate on it—before he kissed her again—almost as if he were reading her mind.

Gigi smiled. If the love and affection of a good man could keep one young at heart, then she didn't think she'd be feeling her age for many years to come.

PAULA KAY

CHAPTER 2

Gigi sipped her coffee on the balcony while she waited for Douglas to join her. She loved waking up in Paris, especially with the incredible view from their apartment. Douglas had planned the whole trip as a birthday gift for her and he'd spared no expense to make it the most incredible week they'd ever had together. Gigi would go so far as to say that if they were to choose a second home in Europe, Paris would easily fill that spot for her.

She pulled her sweater a little tighter around her as she leaned forward to peek through the window, where she could see Douglas with his head bent over his laptop. He must have gotten something important during the night, as he rarely did any work before they'd had their morning coffee together. That was true back home as well.

Their morning ritual was easily one of the best parts of Gigi's day. From the day they'd married, they'd never missed a morning coffee together whenever they were physically in the same place.

She closed her eyes as the memories flooded her.

Their first home as man and wife—the home that Arianna had gifted to Gigi—with all the beautiful mornings in the garden—the very same garden where she and Douglas had been married.

And then there had been the countless mornings in Guatemala—the mornings which would start out quiet enough in their small cottage at the orphanage, only to end up surrounded by laughing children.

And then finally, their quaint little villa in Tuscany. It was there that Gigi had felt a full appreciation of this man that she was growing old with—this man who never rushed her in the mornings—or ever, really, for that matter.

Gigi's eyes flew open at the touch on her hand.

"Oh, sorry, darling—and you looked so serene there. Were you resting?" Douglas sat down next to her and lifted the coffee that Gigi had already prepared for him.

"No. I was just remembering." She smiled.

"Oh? Is it a secret then?"

"No, there are no secrets from you, honey. You know better than that." She reached over to squeeze his hand. "I was just thinking about you, actually—how lucky I am."

Douglas brought her hand to his lips. "I'm the lucky one. Everyone knows that."

They grinned at one another, Gigi enjoying the flirtation.

"So, did you get your work done?"

"Yes, yes. Sorry about that. Just one thing I wanted to handle right away. Now, I'm yours for the rest of the morning, dear. And by the way, what a gorgeous sky. Can you believe the colors?"

"The Eiffel Tower looks incredible, doesn't it? Let's be sure to keep all the info for the apartment. I'd like to show it to Blu tomorrow if she has time to come over. I know she has her normal place she likes to stay, but I doubt it could be as divine as this spot you've found."

"Speaking of Blu and Paris, I hear from Chase that she's doing a lot less travel these days—or at least that's the plan once she finishes her current obligations."

Gigi smiled. She'd talked to Blu about the commitment that she and her husband had made to slow down in terms of how much they were working—how much time they were spending apart from one another. She'd fully encouraged her friend, knowing that their marriage would only end up stronger as a result of the decision.

"Yes, and it sounds like Chase already has his replacement at the restaurant. She tells me that they'll both be able to stay all week after the party." Gigi glanced at her phone as it buzzed with an incoming text. "Speaking of the party—that's Lia. I should phone her. Do you mind, honey?"

"No, not all. You go ahead. Take your time, dear."

Gigi took her coffee and her phone from the small patio table and went inside to sit in the comfy corner chair by the fireplace. Lia answered on the second ring.

"Great!"

Gigi laughed. "Good morning to you too. I'm sorry I didn't get back to you yesterday. Somehow the days seem to easily get away from us here."

"As they should, my friend. Are you having a fabulous time? I love the pictures you've been sending us. I've even gone so far as to put a few hints out there to Antonio. It's been ages since we've been to Paris—or really on any type of getaway. I can't wait until—"

"Until?" Gigi grinned as her friend went silent on the other end of the line. "Do you two have some kind of secret holiday planned? Which would be fine, I might add."

Lia laughed. "Oh no, not really. But we should have in the near future. I need to work on getting that man of mine to agree on leaving the vineyard for a long weekend."

"I'm sure Thomas could help—to look after things if you two want to get away. And you should, Lia."

It was ridiculous but Gigi could actually feel her face getting warm. She thought holidays away—for sure in Paris—had to be good for any marriage.

"Well, I certainly didn't want you to call to talk about my nonexistent holiday plans." Lia laughed. "I just wanted to firm up the menu with you. And you do want it outside, yes?"

"Oh yes, it's the perfect time of year for a garden

party—well, in your case we have an entire gorgeous vineyard as our backdrop, but your garden is quite beautiful as well."

They chatted for several minutes discussing the party menu and a few other details.

"Well," Lia said, "I certainly can't wait to see you—to see everyone. I know that Bella is really looking forward to it too. Jemma and Blu aren't going to believe how big Sam is already. I swear he's grown even since you saw him a week ago."

"Oh, I can't wait to kiss that gorgeous boy."

By the time Gigi hung up the phone with Lia, she was looking forward to getting back home again—but only after she spent two more glorious days in Paris with her husband.

PAULA KAY

CHAPTER 3

Gigi eyed her husband with amusement as he ate the lunch that she'd prepared for them both. They'd spent a relaxing morning hanging around the apartment together, apart from a few phone calls that Douglas had taken—something that was a bit out of the ordinary for him. Gigi didn't press him after he'd gone into the bedroom to take the calls. If she had to guess, she imagined that it had something to do with her birthday—probably a special present, although the trip to Paris had been the exact perfect gift for her.

"How's your salad, honey?" She smiled as she watched him bring the fork to his mouth.

"Delicious. A perfect light meal so that we have plenty of room for this dinner I have planned for you."

"Honey, you do know that you don't need to do one more thing for me for my birthday. This week has been absolutely spectacular and there's nothing else I could possibly need."

"Except for your time with your adoring husband, you mean?"

"Exactly." She got up from the table, kissing his

cheek before she refilled their glasses with water.

"Well, you certainly do deserve any birthday surprises coming your way."

"So, you do know more than what you've been telling me—what Lia and the others are being so hush-hush about? I can't imagine." Gigi laughed. "Honey, please don't let them make a huge fuss. Really. You know it's spending time with everyone that's important to me. I certainly don't need anything fancy."

Douglas reached for her hand across the table. "Oh, they know that—as do I. And you'll love every minute of it. Don't you worry about a thing. Now, what shall we do this afternoon, my love? Any place you want to go? Perhaps one of the museums?"

Gigi thought for a minute. They'd spent their first few days visiting all of their favorite museums—nothing overwhelming—just a few hours each day, but it was the perfect amount of time for her.

"You know, I think I'd like to rest for a bit after lunch. And I owe Jemma a phone call. She's very excited to tell me about the house. They should be all moved in by now."

Jemma and Rafael had purchased a house in the same neighborhood as where Blu and Chase lived—where they'd all been living since the twins had been born. The timing had been perfect and allowed for most of the huge remodel to be done while the family had traveled to Guatemala to finalize everything with the adoption of the two boys.

"Oh, I'm sure they're all really enjoying that. Rafael had shared with me some of the surprises he had for the kids." Douglas smiled.

"You mean that deluxe tree house he had built for them?"

Gigi had loved the idea when Jemma told her over the phone. And the young couple were so excited to have the boys as part of their family. It had been a big change that was yet to go though a lot of adjustments, but she couldn't imagine it any other way after seeing them all together.

"Yes, that tree house is going to be a big hit, I think." Douglas stood up and yawned. "You know, I think a nap sounds like a good idea myself. Come join me?"

"You go on, honey. I'll just clean up here first—maybe see if Jemma's available now to chat—before the kids get home from school is probably better for her."

"Okay, love."

Gigi waited for Chloe to get her mother. The little girl had picked up the phone and chatted a good five minutes with her before becoming distracted by something her twin was telling her across the room.

Jemma was laughing and sounding a bit breathless when she finally picked up the phone.

"Sorry, Gigi. I was downstairs in the laundry room. Tell me all about Paris while I catch my breath."

"Oh, Paris is beyond wonderful, but we can talk about that later. I want to hear all about the house. Does it feel so great to finally be all moved in?"

"It does, yes. Well, of course there is still tons to do. I've yet to finish unpacking and—well, I think I didn't realize how much more laundry there would be with the boys."

She waited while Jemma said something to the girls about going to play in the other room for a little while.

"Honey, is this an okay time to talk?"

"Oh yes, sorry. The girls are going a little stir-crazy. They've had a few days off from their pre-school this week and for some reason they can't seem to remember how they used to amuse themselves—before they had older brothers." She laughed. "Poor Nicolas and Mateo walk in the door after school and don't find a moment's peace until after dinner."

"Aww, that sounds lovely, actually. I couldn't be more pleased over how your family has blended together with the addition of those dear boys."

"They really are sweet. They're so good with the girls—at least for now, anyway. I'm sure, over time, they will need more space than what they're getting right now, but yeah, everything's really good. I can't wait for you guys to come visit so you can see the house. We actually have a guest room now too, so you're more than welcome."

"That's sounds wonderful. I'll talk to Douglas and see

what we can work out."

"Let's talk about it next week—at the party this weekend, I mean."

"Does that mean you all are going to be able to stay a little while? I figured the boys probably have to get back to school, but we would love it if you can stay longer."

"We can't wait to see you. And we're working on it, but yes—I think we're going to take them out of school for the week. We really need to spend the one-on-one time studying with them right now anyway—to help them get caught up—so we figure carving that out while we're away would be a good thing for them."

Gigi could hear Daisy calling to her mom in the background.

"I'll let you go," she told Jemma. "We can catch up later. I just wanted to congratulate you on the move-in and tell you that we can't wait to see your new house— and you, most importantly, I guess, before we see the house."

"Thanks for calling, Gi. Give Douglas a hug from us, and you enjoy your remaining time in Paris. I can tell from your pictures that you're having a blast. And we're all happy for you. You guys deserve the time away."

"Okay, honey. We'll see you all in a few days then. Give big kisses to the kids for me."

"Will do."

PAULA KAY

CHAPTER 4

Gigi smiled across the table at her husband, so handsome in his jacket and tie. Her attraction to him had only grown over the years. The graying hair at his temples perfectly matched his tan complexion, making him look all the more distinguished in her eyes.

He smiled back and reached for her hand across the table. "What is it, my love? You have that look about you."

"Do I? Is it the look that says how much I love you?"

He nodded, and Gigi felt a lump in her throat for loving him so much. He'd truly made her dreams come true.

She looked out the window where they sat, the view of Paris spread out before them as if they'd ordered the magnificence of it off the evening menu. "It's so gorgeous. I know people say this is a bit touristy—eating at the Eiffel Tower—but I don't care. The meal was lovely, wasn't it?"

"I think it was, yes. And I agree. We certainly couldn't ask for a better view. Do you want some more cheese, darling?"

"No, I think I'm saving what little room I have left for one last chocolate crepe on the way home. I will have one more glass of champagne, though." She held out her glass to him as he poured more for her and then himself.

It was her turn to reach across and squeeze his hand. "I don't know how to thank you. This week has been incredible. I can't believe we're actually leaving tomorrow, can you?"

"It has gone fast. Would you stay longer—if we didn't have things to get back to, I mean?"

Gigi thought about it for a second. "I do love it here. So maybe I'd stay a few more days. But really it's the time we've spent together that has meant the most. Let's take that back with us and have many more date nights at home."

"Are you blushing?" Douglas grinned at her—teasing her as he lifted her hand to his lips for a kiss.

"Oh, stop. And probably I am. Don't you feel so special that you can make an old girl like me blush?"

"You are nothing of the sort, my dear. Your beauty only gets more and more ravishing each year that I know you. That's a fact. And speaking of…"

He winked at her as he reached into the bag he'd been carrying all night. "I might just have a little something here for the birthday girl. Now, I know I'm a little bit early with this but I thought tonight worthy of the occasion."

Gigi took the envelope that he handed her and

playfully shook it. "Hmm…well, I don't think it's the new car I've been eyeing or that diamond necklace I saw you looking at the other morning."

He laughed with her. "Open it, my darling."

She loved the lightness of the moment. Douglas knew her well. He knew what really mattered to her, and typically his gifts of jewelry or other expensive items always did catch her by surprise because she was the least likely person to ever ask for anything extravagant. She wondered now if this would explain some of what he'd been up to the last few days.

She opened the card carefully, and immediate tears sprung to her eyes as she lifted the photo that was inside. It was her favorite picture of the two of them the day that they'd gotten married. She was laughing at something Douglas had said, her head back just slightly as he leaned in to kiss her on the neck. In the background, their friends and family could be seen sitting around the small tables that they'd had set up in the garden.

"Oh, honey, I love this picture of us so much."

"I do too. Go on, have a look." He gestured toward the open card.

My love,

I hope that you are ready for another adventure…

For your birthday this year, your friends and I want to take you back to where it all began—where I first met you, where I fell in love with you, and where you made me the happiest man in the world the day that you became my wife.

We all—Lia, Blu, Bella—all your friends and family—
would like to honor you with a birthday celebration to be held in
Marin County, California—in the very same garden where we were
married.

Happiest of birthdays to you, my darling.

All my love,

Douglas

Gigi could feel the tears in her eyes before she fully
understood the meaning of the words in front of her. She
looked across the table at Douglas. "I don't understand."

They'd lived in the house that Arianna had left Gigi
for a while after they were married. Giving it up had been
a logical decision on Gigi's part. By that time, they'd made
the decision to make the orphanage in Guatemala their
home. Gigi hadn't ever really regretted it, but she'd had
pangs of memories over the years for everything that the
house—Arianna's house—had meant to her. And they
had been back—with Isabella for the first time, and other
times when they'd been to San Francisco over the years.
They'd known the owners, and they'd always welcomed
them with open arms.

Douglas was smiling at her, waiting for her reaction.
"George and Vivian are going to be away—actually
they're going to be in Europe for several months—and
they offered the house to me if we happened to be in
town. Of course, this got me to thinking—I know that

the others haven't been back there for so long and—well, Lia actually had the idea of having the party there. What do you think, darling? Is it a crazy idea? Or do you love it?"

Gigi laughed and wiped her eyes with the tissue she'd taken out of her handbag. "Of course I love it! I can't believe it, actually. But wait—when exactly are we doing this? And are you saying that everyone is going to San Francisco?"

Douglas nodded. "Yep, that's exactly what I'm saying. If I remember right, I think we can all manage in the house. I seem to recall at least a few rooms that were barely even used." He laughed. "And actually, I think they've even added a guest house since we've been there last."

Gigi laughed too. She remembered all too clearly how big the Marin house was, because in the early days she cleaned every inch of it. "Okay, so when? Are we still doing the party this weekend—as in a few days?"

"We are—if that's alright with you? Well, everyone's planning to arrive on Friday. And that's when I got our tickets for."

"I can't believe you managed to pull this off. I had no idea this is what you've been planning. You're getting very good at keeping secrets from me, darling." Gigi winked at him.

"So? Are you on board for this weekend?"

Gigi lifted her glass of champagne. "To you, my love.

For still managing to surprise me after all these years. And yes, of course, I'm on board—and very excited."

Douglas touched his glass to hers. "And to you, my sweet—may this be your best birthday ever."

CHAPTER 5

Blu waited anxiously for Gigi to arrive at the cafe. Douglas had mentioned to her that he'd planned to tell Gigi about the surprise the night before, but so far—during their text correspondence—Gigi hadn't mentioned anything about it.

Blu was early for their lunch date.

She'd had one of her last out-of-town meetings only moments before, and she was feeling particularly content about this trip to Paris. It had taken some planning on both their parts, but she and Chase had somehow managed to climb out of what had become a crazy workload. He had resigned as head chef at the restaurant, and she now had a complete team of competent people working alongside her.

The thought of going back to what she loved—the long evenings designing in her work studio at home—was filling her with a joy that she'd not anticipated. Over the years, she'd grown accustomed to all the things she'd had to learn about running her own business—all of the many tasks that seemed to fill up her days to the point where she really had to schedule free time for herself if she needed it. But all of that was about to change, and she was feeling completely at peace about her decision.

She smiled as she checked the photo that Chase had just texted her. It was two tickets that he'd picked up for a new movie release that was playing in town.

Daddy-daughter date tonight, and tomorrow it's your turn!

Blu couldn't remember the last time that Chase and Kylie had been to the movies together. The fact that he'd gotten their daughter to clear her schedule for the evening was saying a lot about the family meeting they'd had before Blu left town. She and Chase had stressed to Kylie that, with her schedule getting more filled up with her modeling obligations, it was going to be more important than ever that they make time together as a family.

At sixteen, Kylie was a typical teenager in most ways, but in others, to Blu, she seemed wise beyond her years. She was extremely thoughtful and honoring of her parents. For the most part, she didn't really give them any cause to worry or not to trust her, so Blu and Chase gave her a lot of freedoms that most kids her age might not have. And now, with her modeling career starting to take off, time would tell how she would handle her continued studies with the workload.

Blu finished sending a text off to Chase just as she saw Gigi enter the cafe.

"I'm sorry you had to wait." Gigi hugged Blu when she stood up from the table.

Blu kissed her on the cheek and grinned at her. "Don't be silly. I'm a full thirty minutes earlier than we agreed on, and I've just been enjoying a lovely cappuccino. And you look incredible, Gi. What have you been doing?" Blu laughed as Gigi's cheeks almost instantly went red. "Okay, or maybe you don't need to tell me everything you've been doing, but I'd say your time in Paris definitely agrees with you, my friend."

Gigi laughed as they both sat down at the table. "Oh, it's such a wonderful city, isn't it? I see why you like coming here so much—well, aside from all your fancy designer friends. And yes, my husband has been showing me a very good time, thank you very much."

Blu winked and took a sip of her coffee as Gigi studied the menu in front of her. "Well, that answer is good enough for me. I'll take care not to embarrass you further."

"I'm not embarrassed—well, okay, maybe just a little, but it's worth it."

They placed their order with the waitress and then Blu reached across the table to take her friend's hand. "So? Tell me everything."

"Oh, you mean about the incredible surprise that you all have been hiding from me?" Gigi grinned back at her. "I really can't believe what you guys have been up to—and Blu, can you imagine how it's going to be—with all of us back in the California house? I never would have even had the idea. For Douglas to think of it—well, it's really sweet."

"It is sweet. And I know what you mean. I'm excited about it too. It will be pretty surreal to be there with Bella—and with everyone really."

Blu didn't miss the look on her friend's face.

"I can guess that you and I—and probably Lia too—have some of the same thoughts about being back there. I mean, don't get me wrong, I'm really looking forward to it. I have so many good memories in that house."

"But there are other memories too—I know. Ultimately, though, I can't think of a better occasion to go back for—and with everyone. I know that would really delight Arianna very much. Can you imagine if she could have known how all our lives would have turned out?"

Blu laughed lightly. "You know, I can and I can't. I think she had a very deep feeling that we would all be okay—and that we would remain in one another's lives. Certainly, she had no doubts about you and Douglas."

Gigi laughed too. "Oh, that sweet girl. Thank goodness for her little matchmaking antics."

Their conversation halted momentarily as the waitress set their food down in front of them.

"Tell me about it. She'd be so pleased, Gigi—at how happy you are—the life that you and Douglas have together. I can't think of a better place to spend such a milestone birthday. I'll tell you what—Kylie, Gabby, and the whole gang of Jemma's is really looking forward to going to San Francisco. I guess the boys just did a school project on the city, and they can't believe that they'll be able to walk across the Golden Gate Bridge in a few days.

"Oh, it will be such fun. I'm glad that everyone is able to clear their calendars."

The two finished their lunch, chatting easily about every topic under the sun.

Blu looked at the time on her phone. "So, are you still up for a little shopping? I've got my whole afternoon free and I think you guys aren't leaving until tonight. Is that right?"

"Yes and yes. I'd like for you to help me pick something new out. I'm thinking for the party, but of course we don't have to go too fancy or anything."

"I'm dying to take you to one of my friend's shops. Her aesthetic is perfect for you and it's not far from here. Let's go find you a birthday outfit, my dear—one that's going to wow that husband of yours—not that he needs any more encouragement in that department, from the sound of things. I think he'd adore you in a potato sack."

Blu heard Gigi laugh from behind her as the two women stepped out onto the sidewalk.

PAULA KAY

CHAPTER 6

Lia smiled at her husband as he handed her a cup of coffee and then put another log on the outside fireplace. The early mornings had been the perfect temperature for her lately, and she loved to spend this time with Antonio before he got busy with meetings and work outside.

Her oasis. That's what their villa was to her. She still had to pinch herself at times, even after so many years, that her life had turned out the way that it had—that she'd actually married the one true love of her life.

Antonio walked back over to where she sat and kissed her on the cheek before joining her on the seat opposite her. "You look very happy, darling."

"Very." She sipped her coffee and looked out over the vineyard. The morning light cast gorgeous colors of yellow and orange across the hills.

"Are you all packed?"

"Almost. Gigi is coming over this morning—to discuss a few party details. Now that she's actually in on the real party, we can go over the remaining questions I have for her. Antonio, I still can't believe that we're going to go back there together—to stay in the house." She reached over to put her hand on his knee. "How are you feeling about everything?"

When Douglas had first told her the news a few weeks ago, her immediate thought was one of excitement for Gigi. She knew how much her friend would enjoy being back there—having her birthday celebration in the same garden where they'd celebrated her wedding. When she'd told Antonio, his somber reaction had made her remember all the rush of emotion that came with the memories of their daughter's last days.

She and Antonio had been back to San Francisco before they were married, but they'd never spent the night in the Sausalito house together.

Antonio placed his hand on top of hers, giving it a squeeze. "I'm okay. Anxious to get there, I suppose. I don't know. There's a part of me that feels like it helps me to know Arianna better, I guess. And you—because I know what that time meant to you—how hard it all was."

Lia was quiet for a few seconds. She'd changed so much over the years. Time had healed her grief, and most of her memories of Arianna were good ones—of the time they'd spent together in Italy and even their last conversations, which had been incredibly sad; but also, Lia now knew how much peace her daughter had found before she passed.

But being there with Antonio? Lia couldn't quite imagine how that might feel.

She leaned over to give him a kiss as she stood up. "It

was hard, honey, and I know the incredible loss that you suffered also—because of me. I think it's wonderful that you'll have this opportunity and I'm glad for the reason— that we can celebrate something wonderful again with Gigi. And on that note…"

Antonio got up from his chair too and they walked toward the house together.

"I should get the rest of our packing done before Gigi gets here so that I can give her my undivided attention. Oh, also, Bella and the kids are coming over for lunch around two. I told her that she could leave them with us for a few hours after—so that she can pack."

Antonio gave her a quick kiss on the cheek. "That's great. I'll just go get my work done so that I'm able to help with the kids after lunch."

Lia grinned at the pictures Gigi was showing her of Paris. It was the first they'd seen of one another since Gigi and Douglas had returned, and Lia was quite enjoying her friend's retelling of the week they'd had away.

She'd finished the bulk of her packing and while Antonio was off at a meeting, she and Gigi were finally catching up with a cup of tea and some much needed girl talk.

"So were you very surprised then? About the trip to San Francisco?"

"I was! I still can't really believe you've managed to

keep it from me this last week."

"Well, it wasn't easy, that's for sure. By the way, what do you think about changing the party to mid-week? I'm thinking the weekend might be rushing it just a bit—we might want a few days to get over our jet lag and relax. And we'll all be there, so maybe there's no reason we can't have it during the week…"

"I was going to suggest the same thing, actually. Yes, let's do that. We'll have more time for some shopping— and Lia, we can certainly hire some help, if you'd rather— with the cooking."

Lia shook her head. "Oh, no. Chase and I are fully on board to create something special for your celebration. Don't you worry about that. We just want you to get there and be nice and relaxed for your big day."

"Well, Wednesday is my actual birthday." Gigi grinned.

"Exactly what I was thinking. So Wednesday it is. It sounds like we're all flying tomorrow. I know Blu had to try to move one thing for their schedule to work, but if not tomorrow for them, she said it would be only a day later—or maybe they'll catch a red-eye."

"That's perfect then. We'll have time to get settled and do some fun sightseeing with everyone."

"Hellooooo!"

They both turned and laughed as three-year-old Arianna ran across the kitchen toward them. Isabella followed her.

"Ari, honey, it's not polite to just walk in without knocking," said Isabella, looking slightly frazzled.

Lia laughed as she leaned down to give Arianna a big hug. "Oh, that's okay, honey. You know I'm always happy to see you."

Gigi stood up to give Isabella a kiss on the cheek and smile at the sleeping baby Samuel that she held in her arms. "May I?"

"Please. I'm dying for a cup of coffee." She laughed and motioned for Lia to stay sitting. "No, don't get up. I'll get it. And sorry I'm a little bit early. Arianna was having a very hard time occupying herself this morning. She's beyond excited about going for a big airplane ride, aren't you, honey?"

Arianna's dark curls bounced as she nodded her head vigorously. "Oh, I'm so excited! Mommy says that I can sit in the seat by the window and I'll get to watch movies on the plane."

"That does sound fun." Lia looked through the window to Antonio, who was motioning to them. "Ari, I think someone would like you out in the vineyard."

Arianna looked toward Isabella, who was back at the table with her coffee. "Can I, Mom?"

"Go on. Go ask Antonio if he needs you to help him with anything."

"I'm on it!"

The women laughed as Arianna ran out the door and across the grass toward Antonio.

"I see what you mean about the energy level." Lia laughed.

Isabella laughed too as she sat down next to them at the small table. "Well, she definitely keeps us busy, that's for sure." She reached out to place her hand on Gigi's arm. "It's so good to see you. How was Paris?"

"Paris was terrific. I'll have to show you some pictures later. Well, I know that you've been there many times, but Douglas got some really cute shots of us around the city."

"It's so magical, isn't it?" said Isabella. "I've been thinking about a trip back there myself. But first we can't wait to go to San Francisco for your birthday. I really think it's going to be a wonderful trip."

"And you've invited Lucas and Kate?"

"Yep, they are beyond excited that we are coming and they said they will be around all week."

"It's a little strange, isn't it? To think of us all gathering there," said Gigi.

"If by strange, you mean wonderful." Lia laughed.

Gigi nodded.

"Oh, it is going to be wonderful. I can't wait to see the house again and actually spend time there. To think of how much has changed since I was there with Thomas the first time," said Isabella.

Lia noticed that Gigi was tearing up a little. No doubt the same flashes of memory were going through her own mind—how much Isabella reminded them of her mother at times and imagining her in the house where Gigi had practically raised Arianna. Yes, there were new memories to be made there. Lia felt sure that it was going to be a good trip for all of them.

PAULA KAY

CHAPTER 7

Gigi felt the tears come as soon as Douglas's arm came around her, pulling her in tight to his chest. The late afternoon sun danced across the flowers and when she closed her eyes, the smells and sounds took her back in time so easily.

"Are you okay, sweetheart?"

"I am, yes. Just taking it all in." She looked up at him. "It feels like it was just yesterday, doesn't it? Our wedding day?"

Douglas smiled and kissed her on the nose. "It does, my love—and you look every bit as beautiful as you did on that day."

They stood in easy silence for several minutes.

"They've done a great job with the garden, haven't they? It's even prettier than when we were here."

"Well, I don't know about that, but it is lovely." He pulled her tight to him again. "What time are the others arriving?"

Gigi looked at her watch. "Lia, Antonio, Bella, and Thomas should be here any minute. I think Jemma and her crew get in very late—like just before midnight. Blu and Chase arrive around noon tomorrow. I figure Lia, Chase, and I can do some food shopping in the morning. Maybe tonight we can order in—from that Chinese place we love?"

"That sounds like a good plan to me. And Lucas?"

"Bella is going to phone him when she gets in—see how the kids are doing after the flight—but I'm guessing he'll at least pop around to kiss those grandkids of his."

"Wonderful. Honey, why don't you sit? I'll go make us a cup of tea."

"Thank you, that sounds delightful actually." Gigi wiped her hand across her eyes, the tears finished, her thoughts clear and peaceful.

Douglas left her to go into the kitchen, and she sat down where she had a clear view of the water below and the Golden Gate Bridge in the distance. How many times had she sat out here with Arianna as a teenager?

She smiled remembering the way that the young girl used to stall when it came to doing her homework after school. She'd grab Gigi by the hand, laughing and telling her how much she'd missed her during the day. "I need my Gi time," she used to say. And then she'd talk Gigi into telling her all about the latest gossip among her friends and get her to recap Gigi's favorite soap for that day.

If Gigi were lucky, before the end of it all, the young girl would give her little glimpses into her life—who was fighting with whom at school and who the latest boy to have a crush on her was. Arianna had never really been that into boys. She'd had boyfriends, but mostly she'd thought the boys at high school very silly—with the one exception being Lucas—and before she'd gotten pregnant. After that point, it had seemed she'd sworn off guys for good.

Gigi looked up to see Bella through the kitchen window just before she opened the door to let Arianna run out to Gigi.

"Gigi! We made it!" Arianna ran across the lawn, followed by sixteen-year-old Gabriela.

Gabriela leaned down to kiss Gigi on the cheek as Arianna settled on Gigi's lap, her head already back against Gigi's chest as she yawned loudly.

"Oh, I'm so happy to see you girls," said Gigi. "How was the flight?"

"It was good, but Ari didn't sleep at all," said Gabriela.

"I'm tired." Arianna yawned again.

"Come on, Ari. Your mom said to say hello and then you're going to have a bath, remember?"

Arianna nodded her head and turned to give Gigi a big hug. "I have to go because I'm really tired. Gigi, it's almost your birthday, you know."

Gigi laughed. "I do know, and I'm so happy you girls were able to come here to celebrate with me."

Arianna reached her hand out toward Gabriela. "Gabby, will you come with me?"

"Yep! Come on. Maybe we can share a room tonight—if our moms say it's okay."

"Yes!" Arianna's enthusiasm for the idea was apparent.

"See you later, Gigi," said Gabriela.

"Okay, honey. Get a good night's sleep, Ari. We have lots of fun things planned for you kids."

"I will, Gigi. I love you."

"I love you too—both of you."

Gigi smiled as the kids went back into the house. Yes, it was a good way to be back there—with a house full of happy energetic children. She wanted to create many more happy memories in the house where she'd spent so much of her life—in the house that already held so many memories, both good and bad.

CHAPTER 8

Isabella ran her fingers over the decorative pillow beside her as she looked out toward the view of the bay. The window seat was so comfy and perfect, as was the entire bedroom suite that Gigi had insisted she and Thomas take for the week. It had been Arianna's bedroom—her mother's bedroom—so many years ago, and although Isabella had seen it once before, to be sleeping there felt more than a little surreal to her.

She smiled when she heard the sounds of Thomas bathing the children in the bathroom down the hall. He'd been quick to take charge of getting the kids to bed, even though Isabella knew that he had to be at least as exhausted as she was. But she knew they'd sleep well tonight. Seeing Gigi's smiling face upon their arrival had reminded Isabella of the importance of the trip and how happy Gigi was that they could all be there with her.

The lights came on in the garden below just as the last rays of light were overtaken by the night sky. Isabella yawned trying to resist the sudden desire to crawl into the bed that looked so inviting. Then her stomach rumbled, reminding her that there was a spread of Chinese food downstairs waiting for them, once Thomas assured her that Arianna was tucked in bed.

She looked up when she heard a light knock on the open door.

"Hi, Gi, come on in."

Gigi crossed the room to sit on the small sofa opposite her.

"I can't believe how little they've changed this room. The furniture is different, but everything is mostly in the same place as Arianna had it." Her eyes went toward the window. "I suppose it makes sense—with the layout of the room. I always did really enjoy this little sitting area—as it looks like you might as well." She grinned at Isabella.

"It is nice. I feel a sense of comfort sitting here already—being in this room—which actually kind of surprises me. Well, not that I would feel that way, but just how it feels to imagine Arianna sitting here. Does that make sense?"

Gigi nodded. "I think it makes perfect sense. You imagine and I remember. And looking at you sitting there—well, it's not difficult to remember exactly what it was like to sit here with your mother. Bella, honestly, you are the spitting image of her."

Isabella smiled. It used to make her feel just the slightest bit strange when people compared her to Arianna. It had always made her feel good, but she thought it made the others sad. Over the years, though, she'd come to find a lot of comfort in the fact that she looked so much like her birth mother. It had become something she was proud of—all the similarities between them.

Isabella turned so that she was facing Gigi. "Is it hard for you? Seeing me here in this room? You can tell me if it is. I'd certainly understand it being weird for you—and Lia."

Gigi shook her head. "No, I like it. It's the way it should be, Bella. Anyway, I came up to tell you that the food is here—whenever you guys are ready. I figured we could kind of just serve ourselves tonight, so I have the guys digging in. It was fun to see Lucas with the kids tonight."

"So fun! He said that Annie is very upset with him for not being able to come, but it's a school night and I guess she has some big exam tomorrow. I told him that she is welcome to spend the night tomorrow if she wants to. I hope that's okay with you."

"Of course—the more the merrier. And we'll make sure that the kids get a lot of time together."

"So, how are you feeling? About your birthday around the corner?"

"Oh, you know, I've not actually spent too much time thinking about it lately. I guess the trip here kinda took my mind off how old I'm getting." Gigi laughed.

"Stop. You're not old at all, and you and Douglas are certainly in fine shape. We should all be so lucky to be as healthy and active as you both are—at any age, really."

"Well, you're too kind but thank you. I suppose I don't feel so old really. Maybe it's true love that does that for a person." Gigi winked. "And if that's the case, you're in good shape with that husband of yours who'll be loving you to pieces for many days to come."

Isabella smiled. "Well, I'd say that Thomas and I sure do have the best role models—for what a healthy marriage looks like."

"You do, yes. And I agree. We're all doing pretty well in that department, aren't we? And what more could I want at my age? Happiness, love, family—I don't think it gets any better." She grew silent, and Isabella didn't miss the change in her expression.

"What is it? What are you thinking just now?"

"Oh, I don't know. About Arianna, I guess. I just wish she could have had the chance to know so much more for herself—for her life. I think she was more content when she passed away than I'd seen her for a very long time, but it's hard to think that she'd never had the chance to know true love or to really know so much of her family—to really know you. If there was one wish— one regret I have for her—it's that she never got the chance to meet you. I think that would have really impacted her life—even at the end."

Now it was Isabella's turn to be silent for a moment. "I know. I've thought about it so much over the years, especially now that I have children of my own. But we're left with the cards we're dealt, I guess." She crossed the short space between them to sit down next to Gigi and wrap her arms around her in a big hug. "And I think having you—having all of you—in my life has been so incredible. I can't dwell on the things that can't be changed. I learned that a long time ago."

Gigi squeezed her tight. "Well, that, my dear, is very well said. It's going to be a great week and we won't start off with any sadness, will we?" Gigi stood up.

Isabella stood up too. "No sadness here."

"I'll go see how everyone's doing downstairs. You and Thomas come down when you're ready."

"Okay, I'll just go say goodnight to Ari and get Samuel from him. I'm sure he's ready for some food himself, so I'll be down just after I nurse him. And Gigi?"

Gigi turned from the doorway to look at back at her.

"Thanks for putting us in this room. I really do love it."

Gigi smiled. "You're welcome, honey."

PAULA KAY

CHAPTER 9

Jemma helped navigate for Rafael as they made their way from the rental car pick-up to the freeway. Arriving close to midnight had its perks, as they'd have little traffic to deal with and would be in Sausalito well before one. She'd told Gigi not to wait up for them, but according to Gigi's latest text, they were all still up enjoying themselves.

Jemma looked toward the back of the minivan and smiled when she saw all four of the kids fast asleep. "They're out—just as I figured they'd be." The kids had watched movies for almost the entire flight—a good thing, as it would be better to get them on California time as soon as possible.

Rafael yawned. "That's good. I'm pretty wiped out myself."

"Do you want me to drive, honey?"

Rafael had stayed on parent duty during the flight so that Jemma could sleep—something she'd been extremely grateful for after having a very busy couple of days prior to their departure.

"No, that's okay. I'll be fine, as long as you keep

talking to me." Rafael reached for Jemma's hand and gave it a good squeeze. "I can't believe that we've finally made it to San Francisco."

"Seriously. How long have we been talking about this? I hope you like it as much as I think you will."

"Do you think it will be hard for you? To be back in the Sausalito house?"

"I don't know, really. I was pretty young, but old enough—I do have a lot of memories of being there—of Arianna playing with me. Whenever she was around, I remember feeling like she was someone magical. I suppose maybe because she was always surprising me with little gifts and things. She loved to do that."

"It's funny—I've heard so many stories about her— about the times you all had here—I feel as if I've been here already. I wonder how it will be for your mom."

"Yeah, I don't know. She seems okay—and excited, actually, but I'm thinking that not all of the memories were so good for my mom. She certainly didn't shed any tears when we left the city to move to the beach—well, not about the actual move anyway. I remember that much."

Rafael nodded.

Jemma had long since told him about her childhood and the secrets that Blu had kept from her. Most of her memories during the time they lived in San Francisco were good, but they'd had hard times too—before her mom had met Arianna. She knew that Blu had worked tirelessly to provide a decent life for them, keeping multiple jobs while also working on her designs when she could steal the time.

They chatted while they drove—about the kids and the things they wanted to do while they were there. The boys were very excited about their first visit to San Francisco, a place that they had coincidently been learning about at school. Finally, after several minutes of driving, their first glimpse of the lit-up Golden Gate Bridge appeared in the distance before them.

"Wow! It really is something, isn't it?"

"It sure is." Jemma opened her window as they approached the bridge. "We'll bring the kids here one day. It's a nice walk across and the view is really spectacular. Well, it is now too—at night—with all the lights." She put her head back against the seat, turning slightly to see the lights of the city spread out before them.

"What is it, honey?"

She felt Rafael's hand grasp hers as her eyes closed and a sudden flash of memory raced through her mind, as present as the cool air now hitting her face. How many times had she made this drive across the bridge with her mom and Arianna? When Jemma closed her eyes, she was six years old again, sitting in the backseat of Arianna's convertible, laughing as the wind whipped their hair and her mom argued with Arianna about the loud opera music that she had playing on full volume. She remembered thinking that Arianna looked like something out of one of her favorite movies about princesses. She'd been so beautiful—like an angel.

"Babe? Are you okay?"

"Sorry, yeah, I'm okay." She looked over at him. "Just a sudden memory, maybe one of many to come, I guess—but not bad." She smiled, squeezing the hand that still held hers.

"I suspect that you'll all be having lots of memories while we're here. I hope it will be good—and not too painful."

Rafael was really one of the most sensitive men that Jemma had ever known, always so in touch with what was going on with those around him. It was one of the things that Jemma loved most about him.

"I think it will all be good." She pointed out the window. "That's the Bay Bridge. It connects San Francisco with the East Bay. Oh, and right down there is Alcatraz. The boys have that at the top of their list. I figure we can do that on a day when we are down by the pier—maybe a cable car ride—all the fun tourist stuff."

The boys—their boys. It was hard to believe that just four months ago, they'd not even known Nicolas and Mateo. And now? Adopting them and bringing them formally into their family had seemed the most natural thing in the world. There was still an adjustment period for them—she knew that they would be grieving the death of their mother for a long time to come—but for the most part, they were doing very well. Their transition from living in Guatemala to Italy had been smooth and they seemed to be settling into their school, with their English—and even Italian—improving every day.

As she was thinking about them, Jemma looked back just in time to see Mateo's eyes go wide as he looked out the window.

"Whoa! It's San Francisco?"

"It is. Look back. Quick! We just went over the Golden Gate Bridge."

"Oh, darn. I missed it."

"We have lots of time, honey."

"How much further?"

Jemma peered down at the GPS app she was following on her phone. "Oh, actually, Raf, it's the next exit, just here."

Rafael drove for a few minutes on the dark road before Jemma pointed again to the left. "There, that's the driveway."

She looked back to see Nicolas awake and asking Mateo where they were.

"Boys, it's very late, so you can say hello to everyone and then we're going to get you all settled in bed for the night, okay?"

Nicolas and Mateo both nodded their heads, looking not the least bit tired.

Jemma smiled at Rafael as they pulled up the driveway to park in front of the house. "I can't believe we're actually here. It looks almost exactly the same as I remember."

CHAPTER 10

While Blu waited for Gigi to join her outside, she walked over to the swing set in the far corner of the yard. She remembered Arianna telling her that her mother had never allowed her to have one while she was growing up—she'd said that it cluttered up the yard and if Arianna wanted to play, Gigi could take her to the park.

Gigi. It had always been Gigi who'd been there for Arianna.

When Blu had first met Arianna, she'd thought it a bit strange that the young girl seemed so much closer to their housekeeper than she did her own mother. But then again, Blu had her own secrets back then, so she never pushed Arianna to talk about her relationship with Mrs. Sinclair. On occasion, though, Ari would tell her bits and pieces—about how Gigi was the one constant in her life—truly the one she went to with anything she needed help with at home.

"It's nice, isn't it? The swing set."

Blu nodded as she looked up to see Gigi walking toward her.

"George and Vivian have it for the grandkids." Gigi held the glass of lemonade out to Blu. "Shall we go sit at the table?"

"Sure."

"Speaking of kids, where'd you say that everyone's gone to?"

"Jemma had promised the boys that they could go do a bit of sightseeing today. Honestly, Chase and Kylie did me a huge favor by insisting I stay home. I'm not sure why they're not feeling the effects of flying all night like I am, but I didn't argue with them." Blu laughed lightly.

"Well, knowing you, I'm sure you were doing a lot before the trip, so better that you get to relax a bit. Let the real tourists lead the troops."

"Bella and Thomas were pretty excited too, so I guess you're right. I forget that they've not really spent much time here at all." Blu reached out to touch Gigi's hand. "It was a good idea to come here. It feels a little strange, but I can already tell that it's going to be good for all of us. How are you feeling, being here?"

Blu waited the few seconds that it seemed to take Gigi to collect her thoughts. She tried to remember the last time that she'd sat with Gigi there. In the moment, she could only recall two distinct memories—the day that Arianna had passed away and the day that Gigi had married Douglas right in the very place where they sat.

Gigi took a sip of her drink. "I feel good, actually—at peace. You know, I'd made my peace with being here—

when Douglas and I made the decision to live in the house. I think I shed enough tears in those first years after Arianna died to last the rest of my life." She laughed lightly when Blu raised an eyebrow at her. "Okay, point taken. I'm still emotional plenty of times. Douglas says it comes with age."

"Well, I think your sensitivity is one of your best qualities, and I don't think that anyone who knows you would disagree with that, so don't go blaming it on age." Blu grinned and reached out to squeeze her friend's hand. "We love you just the way you are, tears and all."

"You're a dear."

The two sat in comfortable silence for several minutes before Gigi spoke again.

"I hope you don't mind that we put Bella in Arianna's room. I did think that you might prefer to sleep there, but—"

"Oh heavens, no. Absolutely Bella should be in there." Blu took a sip of her drink. "Does it feel weird? Being in there? I did take a peek and it's odd how it looks so much the same—almost exactly how I remember it."

"No, not weird exactly. It's mostly very surreal—well, you can imagine. Sitting near the window seat talking to Bella yesterday—if one were just passing by, you'd do a double take for thinking it was Arianna sitting there."

"Yeah, and also to think that Bella has now surpassed Ari in age. I have to catch myself from wondering sometimes—what it would have been like—if Ari was still here—what she would have been like."

Gigi nodded. "Yes. But we can't think like that. We are where we are, aren't we? And largely thanks to Ari, we're in a pretty good place. I for one never dreamed that I'd have this pretty great—slightly crazy—family around me."

Blu laughed. "Ari would love that, you know. I mean, she always wanted a bigger family—people that really 'got her,' she used to say to me. And she'd be especially happy to know that you did bring Douglas into the mix— officially." Blu winked. "You have no idea how badly I wish that Ari could see you two now. Nothing would make her more happy."

Gigi smiled. "Oh, she knew—before any of us. I can still see her smiling about it."

"Me too."

"So, what are the things that you want to do while you're here? It's nice that we have all week, isn't it? And I want to be sure everyone feels free to do their own thing."

"Well, aside from probably doing a bit of the tourist stuff with Jemma and the kids, I'd really like to take her to the old neighborhood one day—maybe just the two of us. She always tells me that the memories of her childhood here are so faint. I thought maybe taking her to some of the places where we used to go might spark something for her—not that all the memories were good or anything, but—"

"Blu." Gigi interrupted her; it was her turn to reach her hand out to squeeze Blu's. "You were a very good mother. We all always knew that. You know, I'm not sure that I ever told you this in so many words, but you taught me an awful lot about not judging people."

"Oh, yeah?"

"I'll never forget that first day Ari brought you to the house—you with your many earrings and bright pink spiky hair. I thought—great, just the kind of bad influence an already slightly out-of-control Ari needs. But then you brought Jemma over, and as time went on, I discovered that you were nothing like that first impression I had of you." Gigi stood up and Blu did too.

"Well, I probably did look a bit wild back then—I was still discovering my fashion sense." Blu laughed.

"You turned out to be the best thing that could have happened to Arianna. I truly mean that, Blu."

Gigi reached out to hug her, and Blu felt the same sense of love and warmth that she'd always felt from Gigi over the years that she'd known her.

It was Blu that had been the lucky one.

PAULA KAY

CHAPTER 11

Lia held Antonio's hand as they walked along the sidewalk toward the cafe that was their lunch destination. She breathed in deeply and looked up at him when he stopped to draw her close. He'd been so patient with her—as he always was—letting her show him things in her time. As she shared the different things that reminded her of Arianna—of their daughter—it was as if she was revealing missing pieces of the puzzle that she'd almost put together for Antonio.

The only other time they'd been back to San Francisco together had been shortly after they'd rekindled their relationship and Lia had still been too fragile, her emotions about Arianna and the pain she'd caused Antonio, too raw for her to revisit much.

He kissed her on top of the head. "I like this part of town. It looks just a tiny bit like home, no?"

Lia smiled. She did like North Beach. It was probably the closest she'd gotten to her childhood memories of Italy before she'd gone back to Tuscany with Arianna. "It does, yes. But the real thing is much better."

"I do like San Francisco, though. I think we should

make a point to come here more often."

"Do you?" Lia liked the Bay Area also, but aside from her memories there with Arianna, she couldn't really see them coming back—not now that everyone she loved lived near them in Italy.

"Well, we'll see, I guess. There are a lot of places I'd like to go with you." He took her by the hand again as they continued walking down the sidewalk.

Lia laughed. "Oh, is that so? Honey, you realize that you're not always so agreeable when it comes to leaving the vineyard." She didn't mind—not really. She loved their home and it was the place she most preferred to be anyway. And Antonio did take time away when it mattered which was any time that Lia asked him.

"Yes it is so, my darling. Hey, I'm trying to take a note from our friends. In fact, I think I've now got that young man who's been helping me to consider doing so full-time. So, you might just have me around the house a lot more than what you want." He winked at her.

"That would never happen." Lia leaned over to give him a quick kiss on the cheek. "I'll take as much of you as I can get—all the time."

They walked a few more steps before Lia stopped outside of the small cafe. This was it. The one place she'd not taken Antonio to yet that held such vivid memories for her. It was crazy how easily she could remember that day as if it had just happened. But it had been a full twenty years earlier that Lia had finally been able to look her daughter in the eye.

Antonio squeezed her hand and watched her. "Shall we?"

She nodded her head and he opened the door.

Lia had read online that the restaurant was still owned by the same family—passed down a generation now—but every bit as Italian as any they'd come across back home. And she could feel that the moment they stepped inside.

The hostess led them to a table near the window and Lia felt her heart beat just a little faster as she looked around the room. It was still late morning and the cafe hadn't yet filled up with the lunch crowd that was sure to be coming soon.

"Shall we start with a coffee?"

Lia nodded. "Yes, that's sound good. I'm not so hungry yet."

The waitress smiled at them as she wrote on her notepad. "I'll have that right out for you."

Antonio reached for Lia's hand across the table and when she looked at him, she had a hard time holding back the sudden tears.

"What? It's okay, my love. It's all okay. Relax please."

She smiled. It was silly to get so worked up about things she couldn't change. Hadn't she learned that by now? One of the greatest gifts that Antonio had given her, all those years ago, was the gift of forgiveness and his forgiveness had been complete. It had taken Lia awhile to realize that. If anything had come between them those first few years together, it was her lack of acceptance of that fact—that Antonio truly had forgiven her for the secrets she'd kept from him. And finally, she'd forgiven herself, only because of Antonio's steadfast love and support.

"You're right. I'm surprised at the way it affects me—being here. I mean, it was so long ago."

"It was, yes. And it was also one of the most critical moments of your life. Why are you so hard on yourself, darling?"

She gave his hand a squeeze. "I love you."

"And I love you. Now tell me about that day—don't leave anything out."

Lia had shared with Antonio every moment with Arianna that she could remember long ago, but it was different being in this place. She knew that it was something he needed to hear again, and perhaps she needed to remember it as well—without the tears, without the judgments and most importantly with the man who'd never let her down by her side. They both deserved that.

The memories were good and in a rush, she let them come—the way Arianna had looked, what they'd ordered, what they'd said to one another…what Lia had felt the day she'd met her daughter for the first time. She'd been filled with such hope after that initial meeting. She knew that it had been the same for Arianna even though she'd later come to know, of course, that Arianna's hopes were different than what Lia's had been for the future.

Antonio listened, encouraging her to tell him every detail. They finished their coffees, moved on to lunch followed by another coffee and all the while Lia continued to talk to him about their daughter, surprising even herself by the odd details that came to her.

"Thank you for bringing me here, honey." Antonio got up from his chair and held his hand out to her.

"Thank you for your never-ending patience with me." She took his hand, stood up and reached her arms around him as she kissed him on the lips. "Today felt good— really good, in fact."

"I'm glad. Now, shall we see if we can find a nice gelato? Of course, I need something to compare to back home."

Lia nodded. "Of course you do dear. That sounds perfect and I think I know just the place." She tucked her arm in his as he led them out of the cafe into the mid-afternoon sunshine.

And Lia felt a little lighter for the memories she'd just shared with her husband.

PAULA KAY

CHAPTER 12

Gigi glanced over at Lia as she placed the tomatoes in their basket. "How are we doing?"

"Pretty good." Lia looked at the list she held in her hand. "We just need to go by the butcher after this, but Chase talked to him this morning and our order is all ready for us. Really, Gigi, you should have let Chase and me finish the shopping. As the guest of honor, you should be doing no work." She laughed.

"Oh, please. I love going to all my old favorite places. I can't actually believe how little has changed since we were last here. Well, there have been changes for sure, but all of our regular spots seem to somehow be surviving despite the changing times."

"And some nice new restaurants as well. Antonio loved the steakhouse you took us to last night."

Gigi felt like the days were already slipping away too fast. There had been some touring with the kids and more than a few good meals cooked at the house together.

Emily and Richard had finally arrived the day before after a delay with their travel plans, and the preparations for Gigi's party the next day were well underway.

Gigi turned to her friend. "That restaurant was good, wasn't it? It was recommended to us by George and Vivian, the owners of the house. There are a few more places I'd like to check out while we're here."

"And what about your friends? Are any of the old gang still around?"

Lia laughed as she asked the question and it instantly brought to Gigi's mind her housekeeping days. It had been a unique time in her life, especially when her role changed after the Sinclairs had adopted Arianna. She'd never really considered herself as a nanny, but everything about caring for the infant had seemed to suit her, and Mrs. Sinclair had seemed so helpless at the time. Gigi could remember that the poor woman could hardly hold the child for fear of dropping her.

She turned her attention back to Lia while they lined up to pay for their groceries. "You know, most of my friends from that time have moved on, I think. A few I've kept in touch with, but they aren't living in the Bay Area anymore. Wow, that sure does seem like a lifetime ago…" Gigi's words trailed off as she noticed a woman nearby.

"Gigi? What is it? It looks like you've seen a ghost." Lia's head turned to where Gigi's gaze had landed. "Do you know her?"

Gigi reminded herself to breathe as she gathered her thoughts. She thought she knew the woman. Could it be? "I'll be right back."

Just as she walked over, the woman turned, allowing

Gigi to see her whole face. It was her. Twenty years had aged her—as it does—but it was definitely Arianna's therapist from all those years ago. The last time Gigi had seen her had been just before Arianna had passed away.

Gigi thought she saw the slightest bit of recognition in the woman's face too, and her brain reached to remember the doctor's name as she stopped in front of her.

"Excuse me. Sorry. You probably don't remember me—wow, it's been so long ago—twenty years, actually, but—"

"I do, but I can't quite place you." The woman smiled.

Gigi smiled too and held out her hand. "Gigi—I was a friend of one of your patients—Arianna Sinclair—I was her housekeeper actually."

It took a moment for her to respond, the shock evident on her face.

"Oh yes. Wow! Sorry. Yes, I absolutely recognize you." She shook Gigi's hand. "Rita—Rita Jonas."

"Dr. Jonas—that's right."

"Sorry. I'm a little taken aback. How are you? Are you still living here?"

Gigi motioned for Lia to come join them. "I don't think you met Lia—that day—well, if I remember right, she wasn't at the house when you came. I'm sorry, I know you probably have had many patients over the years. Maybe this isn't making any sense at all."

Rita reached for Gigi's hand again as she looked her in the eye. "I remember Arianna." And then her attention turned to Lia, who had come up beside them. "Hi, I'm Rita." She shook Lia's hand.

Lia smiled. "Nice to meet you—always nice to meet a friend of Gigi's."

"Lia, Rita was Arianna's therapist," said Gigi.

Now it was Lia's face that went a shade whiter, her shock undeniable. "Oh. Sorry. That caught me by surprise."

"It's very nice to meet you after all these years. Incredible, really." Rita looked from Lia to Gigi. "And here you are together. How wonderful! I must say, it's a bit shocking."

Lia laughed lightly. "I can imagine it's not making very much sense. We live in Italy actually, if you can believe it, but we're back for the week and—"

Lia looked to Gigi, who jumped right in, both of them seeming to have the same thoughts at the same time.

"This is about to get a bit more shocking for you, but I'm going to trust that this is fate—our meeting you here today." Gigi took a deep breath in before she continued. "I know that Arianna told you that she'd given a baby girl up for adoption…"

Rita nodded her head and seemed to be watching Gigi carefully as she continued.

"Well, if you can believe it, her daughter—Isabella—

is now a big part of our lives—along with her husband and two kids—oh—this whole family history might be somewhat interesting to you—if not a bit overwhelming. But we're taking up your time now and—well, it's just really nice to run into you."

Rita laughed and reached out to give Gigi a quick hug. "Are you kidding? This is all just the best news to hear. I'd love to hear everything, actually—to really catch up. Do you think we could exchange numbers? Maybe you'd have time for lunch or something before you go?"

Gigi smiled and nodded when Lia gave her a look.

"Well, actually, we're having a party tomorrow—for Gigi. It's a big milestone birthday for her."

Gigi jumped in. "We'd love to have you, if you're able to make it on such short notice. Wow! It would be pretty incredible for you to meet Arianna's daughter."

"And her father," said Lia.

Gigi laughed at the look on Rita's face. "Lia is married to him, if you can believe it. Oh—and Lucas!"

"You have to come," said Lia.

"Are you kidding? I wouldn't miss this for anything." Rita smiled as she took her phone out so they could exchange information. "Now who's Lucas?"

Lia and Gigi looked at one another and laughed at the same time as Lia proceeded to fill her in while they all got in line to check out.

Gigi was quiet as she and Lia made their way to the car.

"Are you okay, Gigi?"

"Oh yes. I think I'm just a little bit shocked at running into her. Are you?"

"Yes. It's a bit surreal—definitely seems like something that was meant to happen. I think it will be nice to spend time with her."

"And I can imagine it will be pretty interesting for her to put all these faces to names. I know that Arianna had expressed to her most of what she'd told us regarding her wishes. It feels a bit full circle to be able to share that all with her—to share all of you with her."

"You can say that again," said Lia. "Now, shall we hit the last of our list?" She looked at her watch. "I'm starting to get hungry."

"Let's go grab a bite before we pick up the meat. I know a nice little deli just down the road a bit."

"Perfect!"

Lia smiled at her, and Gigi was once again reminded of how much she treasured their friendship. Lia's coming into Arianna's life all those years ago had ended up making a big difference in Gigi's life as well, something that Gigi would always be grateful for.

CHAPTER 13

Isabella chased Arianna down the hall for about the tenth time in the past twenty minutes. "Okay, come on now, Ari. It's time to get dressed for the party. Let Daddy put your dress on and then come in the bathroom so I can fix your hair."

She heard Samuel's cry from the crib in the corner of the room.

"I'll get him," she said to Thomas, who'd managed to get Arianna's dress over her head. "I guess I should feed him before we go downstairs. Honey, Daddy's going to do your hair, okay?"

"That's fine, Mommy." Arianna smiled at her as Thomas fastened her shoe. "Daddy's real gentle when he brushes my curls."

Thomas laughed. "Really? Well, that's very nice to hear—that your good ol' dad does something better than Mommy."

Arianna stood up on the bed and kissed him on the cheek. "Daddy, you're equal. No favorites here."

Isabella and Thomas both laughed at the same time.

"Very good sweet girl," said Isabella while she settled with Samuel in the rocking chair. "Are you excited about Gigi's party?"

Arianna curls bounced as she nodded her head vigorously. "I am. Gigi said there's going to be a special table for all us kids—right by the swing set. Oh, and Mommy—Grandma Lia said there's going to be a surprise for us after we eat."

Lia had hired a magician to come entertain the children, something Isabella knew the ever-curious Arianna was going to love.

Arianna ran over to Isabella once Thomas had placed her down on the floor. "I think Gigi's going to be very happy about her birthday. Mommy, do you have the presents we made for her?"

Earlier that week Isabella and Jemma had taken the children to a pottery shop in town where they'd all picked out special mugs or plates to paint for Gigi. Arianna had taken a lot of care to paint a mug with the Golden Gate Bridge on it. She'd been quite pleased with herself, as were all the children.

"Yes, honey. Daddy will get it for you." Isabella looked up at Thomas. "The presents are in that bag by the dresser there." She reached out to smooth her daughter's hair gently with her fingers as Arianna watched her baby brother nurse. "Honey, go with Daddy in the bathroom to fix your hair."

"Okay, Mommy!" Arianna first kissed Samuel's

blanket and then Isabella on the knee before she ran back over to Thomas, who was waiting with two different bows in his hands.

"Pink or purple?"

"Neither, Daddy."

Arianna's back was to her but Isabella could tell by the expression on Thomas's face that Arianna's little nose was scrunched up as she spoke—something she'd taken to doing just recently whenever she expressed her very strong dissenting opinion these days.

Thomas's eyebrow went up as he seemed to be waiting for his daughter to continue. "Well, then. How shall we fix your hair, my darling?"

"Okay! A little bit of spray, one ponytail"—she turned to look at Isabella—"high up, Mommy?"

Isabella laughed and nodded. "Yes, that sounds pretty."

"High pony—not low—and no bow!" She laughed and then hugged Thomas around the knees. "And thank you, Daddy."

Thomas was shaking his head with a big grin on his face. He looked over at Isabella and mouthed the words "bossy pants" as he started to brush his daughter's dark curls.

Isabella felt a warmth rush through her as she looked first at the cute exchange between her husband and daughter across the room and then to their son nestled contentedly at her breast.

She loved being a mother—much more than she'd ever thought possible. Her children—and husband—had become her life and she wasn't apologetic about it. She'd set her writing aside about midway through her pregnancy with Samuel and the truth was, she wasn't at all sure if and when she'd get back to it.

Luckily, she'd stayed true to her desire to remain self-published. Other than a decent number of fans emailing her to inquire about her next release, her schedule really was completely up to her timing—not that she enjoyed having to tell them that she was unsure. Funny enough, though, even as she had the thought about her family's being worth the lapse, she missed the writing. She had to be honest with herself about that; perhaps it was worth picking up again during the stolen moments of the day when both kids were napping—if she somehow found the energy not to be resting herself.

She looked at Thomas in the doorway with Arianna, her hair and dress looking cute as ever. "I'm right behind you—just going to get myself presentable over here."

Thomas blew her a kiss. "Okay, honey. Take your time."

As Isabella adjusted her top, she looked out the window toward the garden below. They hadn't invited a lot of people, and certainly there were only a few whom Isabella didn't know.

Gigi and Lia had come home from shopping the day before quite excited to tell her who they'd run into. She wasn't sure how to feel about meeting her mother's therapist. It seemed like a reasonable idea, but she also couldn't help feeling anxious about it. It seemed to be her one last connection to her birth mother—the last of the connections that she'd not had yet—and, really, one that she'd never anticipated.

As she looked out the window, she saw Lia giving a glass of wine to a woman. It had to be her—the Dr. Jonas that she'd read about in her mother's journals.

Isabella took a deep breath and wrapped a now content and very sleepy baby snugly in his blanket. "Let's go get this party started, Sammy."

PAULA KAY

CHAPTER 14

Rita smiled as she took the glass of wine that Lia offered her, knowing that it would probably help to calm her nerves a bit. Not that she was normally awkward in social situations, but this event—this intimate gathering that she'd come to realize was made up entirely of the people who'd been connected to Arianna Sinclair, either by blood or by relationship—had totally taken her by surprise. Talk about a blast from the past! Running into Gigi and Lia the day before had been the last thing she'd ever expected.

She'd thought about the young girl—about Arianna—many times since her death. It wasn't often that a patient affected her the way that Arianna had. And running into them yesterday—being here today in the very same place where she'd said her goodbyes to Arianna—was definitely making her feel slightly emotional.

She smiled when she saw a little girl run out to the garden followed by a man she assumed to be her father. She knew even before Gigi came up to her that this little girl was related to Arianna. And before Gigi could speak, Rita's eyes met those of the young woman's in the doorway—just before she handed the baby she held in her arms to Lia.

It was Arianna's daughter. There was no denying the resemblance, and the shock of it took Rita's breath away.

Gigi reached her hand out to the woman, bringing her over to where Rita stood with Thomas and the little girl close by.

"Rita, I'd like for you to meet Isabella—Arianna's daughter."

"Bella, this is Rita Jonas—your mother's therapist."

Isabella reached out her hand. "It's great to meet you. And this is my husband, Thomas—and our daughter, Arianna."

Her smile was wide, and Rita noticed the sweet way that Thomas drew her near him as if by instinct of wanting her close. He picked the little girl up.

"Arianna, say hello to Ms. Jonas."

"Hi. I'm three." She held three fingers up in front of her face and seemed to be admiring her skill at doing so.

"It's nice to meet you, Arianna. What a big girl you are."

Arianna nodded, then turned in her father's arms. "Daddy, can I go play with the twins now?"

"Yes, darling. Play nice."

"I will." Arianna ran off toward the swing set where the other children were playing.

Rita reached over to give Isabella a hug. "I hope you don't mind. It's just—it's so nice to meet you. I can't help staring and I'm sorry. You look so much like your mother. And your daughter—I love the name."

Isabella smiled back. "No need to apologize. It's something I've come to realize—that I look like her and—well, I guess it's been a while since I've seen that look of shock with someone new. How wonderful to meet you, and how crazy that Gigi and my grandmother ran into you like that."

Thomas leaned over to give Isabella a kiss on the cheek. "I'll leave you two to talk." He turned back toward Rita. "It's very nice to meet you. Thanks so much for coming. I know it means a lot to everyone here."

"It's great to meet you too, Thomas. Thank you."

Rita turned her attention back to Isabella, who was gesturing toward a table and chairs under the canopy that they'd had set up in one corner of the garden.

"Shall we go sit?"

"Sure."

Isabella took a glass of juice from a nearby table with refreshments and laughed as they walked to the table. "I'm dying for some wine, actually, but it will be a while before I'm done breast feeding."

Rita smiled. "I saw you do the hand-off to Lia. He's very sweet. Congratulations."

"Thank you. Yes, they are definitely keeping me— keeping us—busy, that's for sure."

"I have to say, it's rather remarkable to meet you—to see your family. Gigi and Lia have filled me in on quite a lot, but I can only imagine what it was like for you to go through your own discovery with everything. If Arianna could have known…"

Isabella seemed to be studying her. Rita had already told herself that she'd let her heart lead her as to how much she would share with Arianna's daughter. Instinctively, she felt that she could trust herself to know what Arianna would have wanted and besides, she already knew about the journals and how much Arianna had opened up to her daughter in giving them to her.

Rita reached across the table to take Isabella's hand. "Your mother wanted everything good for you. I'm sure you've come to know this, but it's important that I tell you that—that you know how much she talked about you to me. There's no doubt in my mind that you were the most important thing to her, especially during those last months of her life."

Rita didn't miss the quick tears that Isabella brushed aside.

"Thank you—for telling me that. I have learned a lot about Arianna—about my mother—through her journals, and also the things that everyone has told me when I first met them and even through the years, really. Just when I think I know all I could possibly know about her, something or someone new comes along, and the picture somehow miraculously becomes even more complete. I think it will be like that meeting you. I'm really grateful for having the opportunity."

She smiled and Rita thought again how much Isabella looked like Arianna. "I'm really grateful too. I think it must be fate."

The two settled into easy conversation, Rita answering questions and remembering things about a time in her life that she hadn't thought about for years. She had mostly retired, although she did still have a few long-time clients that she continued to see on a somewhat regular basis. Yes, she'd known a lot of patients over the years, but none that had had the impact on her the way that Arianna had.

In many ways, Rita felt that meeting Lia and Isabella was more a gift for her, allowing her to put some questions to rest—questions she'd found herself thinking over the years about the young Arianna and what her dying wishes had been.

The time she spent over the next hours in conversation with Isabella, and then later, Lucas, Antonio, and everyone else who'd been such a big part of Arianna's life, only served to solidify those thoughts as true.

Everything Arianna had wanted for her daughter and those she'd loved so much *had* come to pass—the knowledge of which gave Dr. Rita Jonas an incredible sense of peace.

PAULA KAY

CHAPTER 15

Gigi laughed as the kids rushed around her with their presents. Lia had her set up sitting in a special birthday chair that the children had taken great delight in decorating for her. The lunch that Lia and Chase had served was everything she could have wanted for the celebration and now, as the afternoon sun was starting to fade, she knew that she would hold the memory of the day in her mind forever.

She opened the gifts of painted pottery from the children, exclaiming her joy over every piece and feeling the love all around her as the girls fought over who would sit next to her. It meant a lot to her—having them all there.

There were a few more gifts—beautiful candles and chocolates from Lucas and his family, a gift certificate to one of the best restaurants from Rita, and a final large item that Lia placed in her hands.

"It's from all of us." Lia smiled as Gigi started to unwrap the present.

"Oh, how wonderful!" Gigi pulled the framed photo out of the wrapping paper. Earlier during the week, they'd had some photos taken of the entire family in the garden. "I love it!"

"Gigi, see—all the kids are in the front." Arianna gently touched the image from where she sat next to Gigi.

"I do see and I know right where I'm going to hang it, sweet girl." Gigi leaned over to give Arianna a quick kiss on the head.

"In the hallway? By the picture of me and Sammy—and the twins?"

"Nope. This family picture is going right above the fireplace," Gigi grinned as the twins each hugged her from either side.

"I think that's perfect," said Daisy.

"Okay, kids, maybe you can help me pick up the wrapping paper and then I think it might be time for your surprise," said Jemma.

The children dutifully obliged with curious inquiries as to what their surprise might be. Gigi saw Rafael and Chase organizing the magician across the yard and when the kids were done, Jemma led them away.

Gigi noticed Rita watching close by. "It's quite the bunch, huh?"

"Everyone is so wonderful. Thanks so much for inviting me today," said Rita. "I can't begin to tell you what it's meant to me." She walked over, taking the seat next to Gigi.

"Well, having you here—bumping into you like that the other day—just feels like such a right thing. I'm glad it worked out that you could join us. I saw you speaking with Isabella earlier. She's really lovely, isn't she—our Isabella?"

"Oh yes. We had a nice conversation." Rita was quiet for a few seconds as she watched the kids across the yard. "I didn't really know what to expect—how I might feel being here. It's funny, you know. As a therapist, we're taught the importance of guarding ourselves from becoming emotionally invested in our patients—it's not good for them or for us, if we cross that line. With Arianna, that was difficult for me."

"I can imagine—well, you are only human, after all. I'm not sure how a patient's death couldn't effect you, especially one so young."

"Right, but I think it was more than that with Arianna. Of course, I was deeply saddened when she passed away, but—well, I guess I'm talking more about when she was alive. Watching her wrestle with everything she was going through. It's hard not to let that affect one's own thoughts about life. Does that make sense?"

"It does. I think we've all learned something—lots of things—from the tragedy of losing Arianna at such a young age. And I know it's partly the reason that we are all so close with one another. Once you know how quickly people can be taken from you, well—you tend to look at life differently, I suppose."

"Yes, exactly. I had the chance to speak with Lucas earlier too. What a gift for Isabella to be able to have her birth father in her life. I can only imagine what it was like for her—and her parents, really—to suddenly have such an incredible extended family. I can't help but wonder what Arianna would have thought about it all."

Gigi laughed. "We all pretty much agree that Arianna would have been delighted at how things turned out. I don't think she could have imagined a better outcome for Isabella—especially in that her parents—Emily and Richard—are so very supportive and really just as much a part of this family as anyone." Gigi's focus went to where Emily and Richard sat laughing with Samuel nearby.

"That I would agree with." Rita stood up. "Well, I'm going to start saying my goodbyes. Thank you again for having me and the happiest of birthdays to you."

Gigi stood up as well, reaching to give Rita a big hug. "Thank you, and the pleasure has truly been mine."

"You have my number now, so if you're ever back in town, please give me a call. I'd love to keep in touch with you, Gigi."

"I'd like that too."

Gigi felt Douglas's arm around her as she watched Rita walk away. He kissed her on the neck, causing her to shiver slightly.

"Happy birthday, darling. Are you having a good time?" he whispered close to her ear.

She turned slightly to kiss him on the lips. "I am, yes. It's been a wonderful party. It looks like the kids are having fun over there." Her gaze went to where the magician was pulling things out of a hat that had the children in hysterics.

"I'd say so. That was a good idea." Douglas took her by the hand to a little bench in the corner of the garden. "The sky is so pretty. I forgot how beautiful it is here."

"We're pretty lucky, I'd say."

"Well, I know how lucky I am." Douglas grinned as he brought her hand to his lips.

Gigi laughed. "I'm the lucky one—and you know it."

"Agree to disagree." He winked at her.

"I'm glad we're staying here all week. I wouldn't be ready to leave earlier."

"Good. And me either. It's nice being back here, isn't it?"

Gigi tightened her hand around his as she stared across the bay at the bridge in the distance, the sounds of the children laughing in her ears.

"It sure is, honey. I love being back here, actually."

Even as Gigi spoke the words out loud, her feelings surprised her just a bit. She loved living in Italy and wouldn't want to leave, but San Francisco was her home and there was always going to be that feeling about being home that couldn't compete with anything else— especially when home to her involved so many memories of the past.

PAULA KAY

CHAPTER 16

Lia poured the coffee into two cups and waited for Gigi to come out from the kitchen with the scones she'd just baked.

"Wow, that smells delicious. I'm surprised you were up so early to make these this morning," she said as Gigi placed the small plate in front of them on the breakfast table.

"What? Because I'm so old now? I need more sleep?" Gigi laughed.

Lia laughed too. "Well, the party did go quite late last night."

"The party was wonderful. And in case I've not mentioned it, thank you very much—for everything. You all really went out of your way for me and I appreciate that."

"Well, you have mentioned it and you're more than welcome. It's the least we can do for you, Gigi. Truly. I'm glad that you felt special. I—we—always want you to feel that way. You're kinda like our glue around here, you know. You've always done such a great job of getting us all together—both you and Douglas have."

"There's certainly nothing I like better than when we're altogether, that's for sure."

"It was nice that Rita could come. I had a chance to spend more time with her and it was interesting, really—to hear her thoughts about Arianna during that time before she and I first met."

"I can imagine. I think it was great for her to be able to meet Isabella too, and I think Bella felt the same about her conversation with Rita—that it helped her to know her mother even a little bit more. All in all, it was pretty incredible that we ran into her."

"It was." Lia took a sip of her coffee. "So, what are your plans for today? I'm so glad that we're staying on through the weekend. It seems like the days are going by so fast."

"Oh, Douglas and I were talking about a short hike this afternoon. I think the kids are going into town. You and Antonio would be welcome to join us if you like. The weather is supposed to be nice, and I'm trying to hit my list of Bay Area favorites before we leave."

"Does that mean you're heading to Napa?" Lia grinned.

"Ooh, good point. Well, I think we might have to save that one for another time."

"I'll talk to Antonio, but I'm definitely up for a bit of exercise this afternoon. Thank you."

"I'm all ears." Antonio grinned from the doorway. "In fact, my ears were burning, I guess."

"I know how that goes," said Douglas from right behind him.

"Douglas, grab coffee cups and a few more of those scones and come join us," said Gigi.

"Gigi was just asking me if we wanted to join them for a hike this afternoon," Lia said to Antonio as he sat down beside her, kissing her first before taking a big bite out of his scone.

"That sounds like a good plan to me. Do the kids need our help with anything? All the little ones are accounted for today?"

Lia loved how helpful Antonio always was when it came to caring for the children. She knew that it was an experience that he hadn't ever thought he would have. He and Samuel had quite a bond, which was something that warmed both Lia's and Isabella's hearts.

"I'm pretty sure that they are all going into the city today. I heard Bella talking to Jemma about wanting to take the kids to the park," said Lia.

Douglas scooted his chair in near Gigi, taking her hand under the table, and then he turned toward Lia. "There's this lake that we always used to love to walk around—not too far away—I think you'll really enjoy it."

"Well, that's settled then. And Lia and I would like to take you two to lunch, so if there's a spot you like near where we're going, keep that in mind," said Antonio.

"It's so quiet," said Gigi. "I can't believe the kids aren't up yet."

"I think they were up pretty late last night. I heard the boys giggling next door to us way past midnight," said Lia.

Gigi laughed. "Well, good that they're sleeping in then."

"I'm not so sure about sleeping in," Blu said from the doorway, causing them all to turn to look in her direction. "I swear, it was the smell of these scones that woke me up. May I?" She gestured toward the plate on the table.

"Yes, yes. Pull up a chair," said Gigi. "Honey, let me get you a cup of coffee."

"No, no. Sit. Please. I'll get up in a minute. I just want to sink my teeth into one of these."

Gigi was watching her with a funny look on her face.

"What is it, Gigi?" said Lia. "Are you okay?"

Blu had a look of recognition on her face as they all waited for Gigi to respond. It was one of those moments that Lia had seen before—the history of being in this house, the memories that they both shared. How many times had Gigi made scones for Arianna and Blu those last years before Ari died?

Gigi seemed to have collected her thoughts. "Yes, sorry, I'm fine. Just a little flash of memory there that took me by surprise for some reason, Blu—watching you just now, complimenting me on the one thing that I used to make that was even edible."

Blu laughed. "That's not exactly true, Gigi—well, true that we loved your scones, but we loved other things as well."

"Like?"

"Uh—like the chicken salads that you used to make for us. And the tea and cookies in the afternoons sometimes."

Gigi turned toward the others. "Store-bought cookies."

Blu got up to come around the table and put her arm around Gigi's neck. "But anyway, you know we never cared about that. We loved being around you then—Ari and I—just as I love being around you now." She leaned down to kiss Gigi on the cheek.

"As do we all," said Lia. And she could hardly remember what her life had been like before she'd known Gigi and the others—before she'd known her daughter.

PAULA KAY

CHAPTER 17

Blu waited in the car for Jemma to finish saying goodbye to the kids. The two of them were going to go into the city to check out their old neighborhood. Rafael, Bella, and Thomas were going to meet them at the bridge with the kids later, as walking across it was the one big thing they'd not done with them yet.

"Okay, girls, be good for Daddy. I'll see you in a little while," Jemma called over her shoulder to the twins as she made her way to the car. "They have so much energy today. Poor Rafael." Jemma laughed. "Oh well, the boys sure are excited about finally walking across the bridge, so they have that to look forward to."

Blu started the car down the long driveway. "I'm glad this worked out, honey. It feels like it's been a while since you and I have had some time together—just the two of us." She reached her hand out to take Jemma's.

Jemma smiled and rested her head back against the seat. "Me too. It's a good idea—while I have all the help with the kids."

Jemma's eyes were closed, and Blu glanced over at her before she turned the car onto the highway. She seemed happy but also a bit frazzled. Blu worried about her. Having their family expand so suddenly with the adoption of the two boys was no easy thing. How could it be? But also, Blu knew her daughter well enough to know that she'd do anything for her family—for Rafael. And it had been more than apparent at Christmas that the boys had won over both their hearts.

"What?"

Blu laughed, because Jemma's eyes were still closed as she spoke.

"Huh?"

"I can feel you staring at me." She opened her eyes and sat up a bit in the seat. "Sorry, I guess I'm a little tired. Maybe we can stop and get a coffee?"

"For sure we can. We'll see if any of my favorite cafes are still there—in our old neighborhood."

The words echoed in her head after she spoke. The old neighborhood she was taking Jemma to—the only one that Jemma remembered—was where they'd lived once Jemma was around two years old. Before that, when Blu had first arrived in San Francisco with infant Jemma, things had been pretty grim.

Blu would not be returning to that part of town. She'd scrimped and saved and practically worked herself ragged to be able to afford rent in a neighborhood where she could safely take Jemma to the park. Yes, those early days had been hard; Blu remembered constantly having to look over her shoulder. Living with secrets could destroy a person, and she'd done whatever she could to rise above that for Jemma's sake. Everything had been for Jemma, and Blu had no regrets when it came to those early decisions she'd made.

"Mom?"

"Sorry, yeah?"

"You're totally zoning out there. Do you want me to drive?"

"No, sorry. Just thinking."

"About?"

"About how it's been to be back here. What does Rafael think?"

"Raf loves Marin. He thinks it's really beautiful, but you know, he's so not one for busy places."

"But he does like where you are now, doesn't he?"

"Florence? Yeah, sure he does, but I don't think he'd like living in the city center or anything. He's definitely more of a quiet neighborhood kind of guy. But yes, he and the kids are really enjoying themselves. Chloe and Daisy have already been begging us to stay longer."

"That's a good sign. I'm glad the kids don't seem to be bored here. Having the nice yard helps, I think. And you have been taking them to a lot of fun places."

"Speaking of, where's Kylie gone to? Last time I talked to her she told me that she was going to a party in the city—some designer's house and a few friends that happened to be in town?"

"Yes, true. One of her friends that she met through

work lives in San Francisco." Blu glanced at the time. "She should be back soon, actually. Chase was going to pick her up."

"Well, I've hardly seen her—or spoken with her now that I'm thinking about it—since she started the modeling."

Blu could feel Jemma staring at her.

"Are you okay with how busy she is? What's going on with school?"

"We're still working all that out—and I'd be lying if I said I didn't have any feelings about it—I don't want it to interfere with her school or family, that's for sure." Blu glanced over at Jemma. "But you should see her. She's really so good."

Jemma smiled. "Kylie's gorgeous. I always knew that she'd end up being a model." She sighed. "I just—I don't want to lose her, ya know—to that whole world."

"We won't, honey. I'll have a talk with her when we get back tonight. I think she's planning on spending the rest of the week with us. I know that she and Gabby have some plans together."

"I just miss her—as do the girls, of course."

Blu drove in silence until they approached the Golden Gate Bridge.

"The sky is so clear today. It's a perfect day to come for a walk."

"It's so pretty," said Jemma as she looked out the window across the bay.

"Do you have memories of us driving across when you were young?"

"I do, yes. Usually when I think about it, I imagine Ari's convertible and that loud music."

Blu laughed. "That awful opera music she loved so much."

Jemma laughed too. "I remember kinda loving it."

"I'm glad you have those memories—that you can remember her. I think knowing you—spending time with you—was really healing for Ari."

Jemma was quiet for a few minutes. "I think about Ari—and Lia—now that I'm a mother myself. I can't imagine ever having the strength to do what they did—to give up my babies." She glanced quickly at Blu. "But I don't mean that in a judgmental way. I know that they were doing what they thought was best for their babies—I get that. I just—I just can't imagine the pain that it must have caused them."

"Well, let's just be thankful that life gives us opportunities to heal and move through that kind of pain. I think that both Arianna and Lia were able to do that."

"And let's not forget that I am just lucky to not have ended up in such a situation. I do realize that my life could have ended up very differently—were it not for you—and Gigi and Douglas. I really can't believe what a little jerk I was when I was younger. I'm not sure how you and Chase ever survived that."

Jemma laughed lightly but Blu knew the seriousness

of her statement, as they'd talked about that time in her life many times before. Jemma had more than made her amends to them and once she'd made the decision to change her life, there had been no turning back for her.

"Well, we sure do have a lot to be thankful for, don't we?" Blu turned the car into the parking lot of what used to be her favorite coffee spot—miraculously still there. "Now, let's see about getting a coffee and something sweet to eat before I take you on this tour."

They got out of the car and Jemma walked around it to embrace Blu in a big hug.

"What's that for?" said Blu.

"We do have a lot to be thankful for and I'm especially thankful for you."

CHAPTER 18

Jemma walked arm in arm with Blu. After they'd driven past their old apartment building—or at least where the old apartment used to be—Blu had wanted to stop at the park where Jemma had spent hours playing as a child. And the park was spectacular.

"I'm kinda bummed about the apartment building," said Blu. "I can't believe how built up that whole neighborhood is now. When we lived there, it was all pretty much residential."

"Are you surprised?"

"No, I guess not. Not really. I am surprised about this park, though. When I used to bring you here, it was really hardly more than a small patch of grass, a merry-go-round, and a few swings. Do you remember, Jem?"

Jemma scrunched her nose as she looked over at the children playing on what was now an elaborate climbing structure. "I'm not sure. I mean, I think I do, but it's all kinda jumbled up with our move to the beach, I guess. But I definitely do remember you taking me to the park— and this one is really great, actually."

Jemma's phone dinged with an incoming text.

"Is it Rafael?"

"Yes, he says that they'd be ready to leave for the bridge in about an hour if it's good for us. Was there anything else that you wanted to do?"

Blu was quiet for a minute and Jemma got the feeling that there were more places that she wanted to take her, more things that she wanted to tell her.

"Maybe one more stop—a quick one."

"Okay, any hints?"

"Nope. Let's go!"

They walked back to the car and Jemma sent Rafael a quick text. "I'm telling Rafael that we'll meet them in the Marin side parking lot in about two hours." She laughed at the funny look on Blu's face. "I kinda have a feeling that our stop might not be as quick as you anticipate."

Blu laughed. "That, my dear, is probably a good call."

Blu pulled out of the parking lot and they started driving toward downtown.

"Okay, well, I see that you are definitely taking me somewhere that is not in our neighborhood."

"Yes, that would be right."

They crossed busy Market Street and Blu peered intently down a few of the cross streets as she drove slowly. "Let's see if I can even remember…here. Wow! I actually can't believe it's still here!"

"What? Where are we?" Jemma laughed as she looked around at the street, semi-quiet except for what looked like a few small bars and eating spots.

Blu pulled into a small parking lot behind what looked like a completely out-of-place bar.

"Ah ha! The hole-in-the-wall?" Jemma grinned at her mother.

"The one and only. I think it's only fitting that I treat you to one drink in the place that started everything—the place that changed our entire lives, really."

Blu was joking but Jemma knew that there was a lot of validity to her statement. Blu had met Arianna one random night when she'd happened to come in the bar for a drink. And meeting Arianna *had* changed their lives—it had changed everything.

Jemma grinned as she slammed her car door shut and followed Blu across the lot to the entrance of the bar.

"Well, this ought to be interesting."

Blu turned toward her and winked. "Thanks for humoring me today. I do appreciate it."

"Don't be silly. The only humorous thing is that you crack me up." Jemma reached for her hand as Blu opened the door. "It's been a fun day. Really fun."

"Wow, it's quite dark in here." Jemma followed Blu to the bar, where they sat down on a couple of stools.

Blu laughed. "Funny, it's just how I remember it. A bit depressing, isn't it?"

Jemma looked around the room. Considering they weren't exactly there during happy hour, it was hard to imagine if the place would look any different with a crowd of people filling its space. There was a lone guy sitting at the end of the bar who looked as if he'd been there all day. And there were two young guys playing a game of darts in the far corner of the room.

Jemma smiled at the bartender as he came over to them.

"What can I get for you pretty ladies?"

Blu looked at Jemma. "We probably shouldn't have actual alcohol, right?"

"Do you mean because you are driving or because you're going to hang out with my pack of kids after this—which, I might add, could be an argument for alcohol, not against it."

Blu laughed. "Well, I don't know about that but I'll have a diet soda, please."

"I'll have the same, thanks," said Jemma.

Jemma didn't drink much—not since she'd learned the lessons of bad decisions during her youth—so it was interesting to her to even be sitting in a bar.

After the bartender delivered the sodas, Blu raised her glass for a toast. "To memories, good and bad, that shape our lives and make us better people." She closed her eyes for a moment before continuing. "And to Arianna—for walking into this awful place twenty plus years ago."

"To Arianna." Jemma smiled and reached over to squeeze Blu's hand. "Now tell me again about the night you two met here."

CHAPTER 19

Isabella pulled her hoodie a little tighter as she walked with Lia along the pedestrian walkway that spanned the length of the Golden Gate Bridge. Blu, Jemma, and Rafael were walking ahead of them with eyes on the laughing children, who were excited to finally be making the trek across the bridge.

"It's always been amazing to me—how cold it can be in this spot. No matter the weather, you pretty much always need a jacket or something," said Lia.

"Yeah, I'm glad I brought my sweater. It's so pretty, isn't it?" Isabella had not spent that much time in San Francisco, although she had been there a few times to visit Lucas.

"It sure is," said Lia, stopping at the midpoint to admire the view across the bay.

"Did you used to come here a lot?" asked Isabella.

"No, not really—only when I first moved here and then a few times with Arianna. She really loved this bridge—walking across it, driving across it—it didn't matter. Something about it just seemed to make her feel better. I suppose maybe it was the familiarity of it. When she would talk about wanting to travel, she always did so with the additional comment that San Francisco would always be home to her."

"That's a funny thing about travel dreams, isn't it?" said Isabella.

"What's that?"

"Well, ever since I was a young girl, I had this mad desire to travel. And I actually never knew to what extent I'd be able to. So, after it's all said and done, I think I feel about Tuscany the way that Arianna felt about here. It's become my home now. I really can't imagine living anywhere else."

"I know what you mean. I think it's our Italian genes." Lia smiled at her.

"Yeah, and maybe I'd feel differently if my parents were still out east, but I don't know. I think it would still just be a place to visit. And let's face it, what's not to like about Italy, right?" Isabella grinned.

"Oh, I agree about that sentiment, especially since you and your gorgeous family live five minutes away from me." Lia reached over to squeeze her hand. "I can't imagine being separated from you now, so please don't get any big ideas—not while I'm still around anyway."

"I don't think you need to worry about that. You know how happy Thomas and I are there—and besides, I'm pretty sure you are going to be around for quite some time, so don't be getting any big ideas yourself."

"Deal."

"How are you feeling about leaving in a few days? It's gone fast, hasn't it?"

"Yes, it has. I'll be ready to get back to the vineyard, I guess. Mostly because I know you all are going back too. And of course Antonio is enjoying himself, but I know he's itching to get back to work."

"The kids sure are having fun." Isabella waved to Arianna, who was shouting hello to her from several feet ahead of them. "I think Arianna would be happy anywhere as long as she had the twins for company. It's going to be a rude awakening when they are separated again next week for a while. I guess I might have to prepare her for that."

Lia nodded. "I'm sure it won't be long before the kids see each other again. And what do you think about Gigi? It seems like she's been enjoying herself, don't you think?"

"For sure. She was so happy with the party. And I know she's talked to us both about how good it feels to be staying in the house. I tend to forget how long she lived there—her living in Italy just feels so natural—so when I think about that, it's a reality check that maybe this does feel like home to her. What do you think?"

"I think you might have a point. It's hard to know sometimes how it's going to feel to be in a place that holds such memories. It's something I can relate to from being back in Tuscany and also being back here. But over time, I think the good memories far outweigh the bad. That's how it seems for me anyway. I can imagine it's similar for Gigi."

"Well, she doesn't seem sad this time—not like what I've seen in the past or what I might have expected."

"I'm sure she's been a little preoccupied too—with her birthday and everything," said Lia.

"She's okay with turning seventy, isn't she? I mean, I know she's joked about her age a lot lately, but honestly she and Douglas don't act their age at all. I could only hope to be like her when I'm seventy." Isabella grinned and looked at Lia. "And I'd say there's a pretty good chance of that only because I'm lucky enough to have your gorgeous genes."

Lia leaned over to give Isabella a big hug. "You're too kind, my dear. Now, shall we catch up with the others— maybe turn our rather slow stroll into some actual exercise?"

"As in, you're up for a jog?" Isabella missed running. She'd been out of her regular routine with it since midway through her pregnancy with Samuel. Maybe she'd be able to steal away one morning before they left to have a good run across the bridge. She laughed at the face Lia was making in reaction to her suggestion that they jog. "What? You might try it, Lia."

"Would you settle for speed walking?" Lia laughed.

"You're on. Let's go!"

CHAPTER 20

Jemma lay back against Rafael's chest on the small sofa in the room where they were staying. Gigi had put them in the master suite, which at first Jemma had objected to. But she'd been so insistent and the room really was very nice. With the boys in one room down the hall and the twins in the other, her family officially now took up one wing of the large house.

Jemma's eyes closed but then just as quickly opened again as the sounds of shouts and running children down the hall met her ears.

"Raf, how are those kids not tired? I simply don't understand their energy. I really would have thought that walking—well, mostly running for them—across the bridge would have tired them out today. It sure did me."

Rafael laughed. "Hey, I know what you mean. It's like being outside literally recharges their batteries or something."

"And why does it have the opposite effect on me?" Jemma leaned up to give him a quick kiss on the cheek. "Today was fun, though. I think the kids are really having a good time."

Jemma felt Rafael smooth her hair back from her neck, the soft graze of his fingers making her shiver.

"And what about you, darling? Are you having a good time? How was the time with your mom?"

"It was good—really good, actually. I have the feeling that it really meant a lot to her today—going down memory lane together. I'm not sure why we've never done that here before—well, not to that extent—but it felt nice."

"Your family is so interesting."

Jemma laughed lightly. "Is that a nice way of saying that my family is so weird?"

Rafael kissed her on top of the head and laughed too. "No, silly. Not weird at all. I just think that the connection you all have is really something."

Jemma sat up so that she could look at her husband. Rafael didn't talk about his past much—about what life had been like for him before the orphanage—but he didn't have to talk about it with her for Jemma to understand that his life as a young boy had been rough. She knew what living at the orphanage had done for him—what Gigi and Douglas—and Silvia, before they'd taken over—had meant to him.

Jemma looked into her husband's eyes, willing the intensity of her words to hit his heart.

"Honey, just in case you were to ever have any doubt, you are also a part of this crazy family—a big part. You're like a son to Gigi and Douglas, you do know that, don't you? Anyone can see how they care about you."

"Oh, I know. I didn't mean anything by it. Well, nothing depressing. I just notice how it seems to be affecting the others—to be here. Especially Gigi and Lia. And I can understand that." He pulled her back down to his chest. "Now lie with me for a little while. Let's try to close our eyes for a minute while the kids seem to have quieted down a little."

Just as Jemma closed her eyes, a ball landed on the floor just beside them followed by the eruption of Nicolas and Mateo into the room.

"Boys!" Rafael's voice wasn't overly loud but Jemma knew he meant business. "No playing ball in the house."

"Sorry. Sorry." Mateo put his hands up when Rafael and Jemma looked at him and then he looked over at his brother, who already had the ball in his hands. "Nicolas— here. Toss it to me."

Before Rafael could scold them again, Nicolas sent the ball hurling over the sofa—probably harder than what he'd meant to—where it thudded to the floor followed by a yelp from Mateo as he tried to catch it.

"Ow, something's wrong with the floor over here. Oops, I'm so sorry, guys. I think the ball broke the floor."

"Oh wow. You are so in trouble, Mateo—right, Mommy?" Chloe said as she and Daisy ran over to where the floor seemed to be buckled up underneath a small rug.

Jemma and Rafael got up quickly and crossed the room.

"Well, we don't like that you boys are playing ball inside. No more of that, okay?" said Jemma.

The boys nodded.

"Now, back up just a bit, let me take a look. This is very odd." Rafael slid the rug over to the side. "Oh, it looks like one of the boards just came loose here. The ball must have hit it just right or something." He pulled the single board so that it was all the way out. "I can nail that back in, no problem." He turned toward the kids. "You guys stay away from this spot until I get it fixed. In fact, please go play in your rooms for a little bit."

The kids left and Jemma knelt down beside the small open space in the wood flooring. "Rafael, can you shine your phone here, please? This is so weird, but I swear I can see something in there." Rafael turned his flashlight app on and Jemma pointed into the space. "There, do you see that bit of red?"

Rafael nodded and wiggled the board next to the opening left by the one that had come loose. He reached inside and pulled up what looked like a very old book. "Jem, I think we've just found a secret hiding place."

Jemma's heart starting pounding faster the moment Rafael removed the second board. What was it? Whose was it?

It was a journal. She knew it without opening it.

She reached out to put her hand on top of the closed

book sitting on the floor in front of them and when she spoke her voice was barely a whisper. "Wait. I'm going to go get Gigi."

PAULA KAY

CHAPTER 21

Lia was just settling in on the sofa with Gigi when she heard footsteps running down the stairs in the other room.

"Gigi? Douglas? Gi, where are you?"

It was Jemma, and Lia could tell by the sound of her voice that something wasn't right.

"We're in here, honey," said Gigi and then she—like Lia—saw the expression on Jemma's face. "What's wrong, Jemma? Are the kids okay?" Gigi stood up from the sofa. "Douglas is out running an errand, but I can call and get him right back here."

"No. No, sorry. Everyone's fine. I just—Rafael and I stumbled upon something—in the bedroom."

"What do you mean stumbled upon something?" Gigi turned to Lia. "That sounds mysterious, doesn't it?"

Lia nodded and stood up too.

"Okay, well, let's go have a look," said Gigi, gesturing to Lia to come too.

The two followed Jemma upstairs and when they entered the room, Lia could see Rafael sitting on the sofa in the corner of the room holding something on his lap.

"So the kids were playing kinda rough and all of a sudden one of the floorboards come loose. I could just barely make out the red of the book—well, you can see how faded it is—but it looks like a journal, doesn't it?"

Gigi walked around the sofa to sit next to Rafael. "May I see?"

"Yes, sure. We didn't look inside. Jemma thought it best if you were the one to look." Rafael placed the book in Gigi's lap and she careful opened the cover.

Lia watched and waited as Gigi seemed to quickly skim a few pages. Then her face went pale.

Jemma reached out to touch her on the arm. "What is it?" she whispered.

Gigi shut her eyes for a few seconds before she spoke. "The journal seems to belong to Mrs. Sinclair. I— I'm sorry. I think I'm going to need a little time alone with this—to talk to Douglas about it. Please don't take it personally. It—well, it seems very private in nature."

"Don't worry about us. This is not our business," said Lia.

Jemma added, "That's right—well, not that we're not curious or anything, but like Lia said, it's certainly not our business. I actually thought—I was hoping—that it might be a journal of Arianna's."

Gigi shook her head and got up from the sofa, the worn book in her hand. "No. No, it's definitely not Ari's. I'm just going to go give Douglas a call now."

Lia gave Gigi a quick hug before she left the room.

"Let me know if you need anything."

"I will, thanks."

Once Gigi had gone, Lia walked back over to the sitting area by Jemma and Rafael. "Well, whatever is in that book definitely shocked her. I hope it's nothing horrible."

She saw Rafael reach for Jemma's hand and give it a squeeze.

"Me too," said Jemma. "I kinda thought the family was done with big secrets—as many as we've had among us."

"Hmm—funny that you all are talking about secrets the moment we appear," said Blu from the open doorway with Isabella right behind her.

"That's either a cue for us to leave or to come in and bug you until you spill the beans." Isabella laughed. "Wait! Jem, you're not pregnant, are you?"

"Oh, no way."

Rafael looked at Jemma in a way that made her laugh.

"Well, maybe I shouldn't say it quite like that, but I'm definitely not pregnant."

Rafael leaned over to kiss her before standing up. "And I think that's my cue to leave you ladies alone. I'll go get the kids going on dinner."

"Thank you, honey."

Rafael left and Isabella took the space where he'd been sitting on the small sofa. She looked from Jemma to Lia. "So what's going on? Is everything okay?"

Lia locked eyes with Jemma, wondering how much they should say. Jemma nodded. Gigi would decide what she wanted to share about the journal, and Lia didn't think she'd mind them sharing the discovery with the others.

"Raf and I found an old journal under the floor—well, we didn't know for sure it was a journal, but Gigi just confirmed that when I called her in here to show her."

"One of Arianna's?" Isabella asked and Lia could see the hope in her eyes.

"No, honey. It didn't belong to Arianna." Lia glanced at Jemma again before she continued. "I think we should wait for Gigi. She wanted some time alone with it."

"How mysterious—and how strange to find it after all these years," said Blu.

Lia was thinking the exact same thought, and her mind was swirling when she recalled the look on Gigi's face as she'd skimmed the journal.

Something Gigi had read in it had definitely surprised her and by her reaction, it wasn't exactly a welcome surprise.

CHAPTER 22

Gigi waited for Douglas in their bedroom. Her hands shook as she reread the journal entries for about the tenth time. There were only a handful of them but they seemed to span a period of about five years—each one offering a glimpse into a woman that Gigi had never really known, despite the fact that she'd lived in the same house with her for over twenty years. This reality stunned Gigi.

The first entry had been shocking to her for the simple fact that in it, Mrs. Sinclair had written about her therapy sessions and the encouragement of her therapist to begin writing in a journal—that it would help her to give voice to some of the deep emotional wounds that she was suffering from. She wrote about keeping secrets from her husband—that he didn't know that she'd been seeing a therapist and that it wasn't anything she could ever tell him. She knew how to be the picture-perfect wife to her successful husband, and having an emotional breakdown certainly did not fit that ideal image.

It was the second entry that had made Gigi's heart beat wildly. This was not anything that she would have ever imagined, although she found herself grabbing at very old bits of memories—of incidents during those first few years of her employment with the Sinclairs—things that she might have thought odd at the time, but pushed aside because it wasn't her business as the hired help. Her eyes flew over the words again. They were words of panic and despair.

What have I done?…How could I have let him talk me into killing my child?…God is punishing us…I hate him but more than that I hate the evil man who did this to us. I feel dirty. He says he knows it's not my fault but he blames me. I can see it in his eyes when he tries to make love to me. I should have had the baby. I should have been strong enough to leave him. Please God, if you could give us a child…forgive me for my sins.

Gigi took a deep breath and finished reading the entry. She didn't say it outright in her written words, but Gigi felt confident that this was the heartache of a woman who'd been raped. A rape that had resulted in a pregnancy.

And Mr. Sinclair? Was it possible that he'd been so unsympathetic to his wife's pain? It wasn't the way that Gigi had ever thought of him, but the words on the paper painted the picture of a husband whose answer to the issue of the resulting pregnancy was to get rid of the evidence—the child.

Gigi tried to imagine it—what an impossible situation to be in—for both of them. Yet, the thought of them going through with an abortion was truly shocking to her.

She could now piece together the years that followed. Though they certainly didn't share a lot about their personal lives with her, she knew all about the time period of their trying to get pregnant. She remembered the moodiness of Mrs. Sinclair and nursing her after the two miscarriages she'd had.

God is punishing us…

Gigi's eyes were drawn back to that section on the page. It was no wonder that the woman had thought that. She remembered the despair and depression during those months.

A few entries later, there was a change in tone. Mrs. Sinclair had talked about their decision to adopt and the hope that she felt it was bringing to their marriage. She'd been trying to fully forgive her husband for the past, and his willingness to even look at the option of adoption seemed to be a concession on his part—a way for him to ease his guilt, perhaps. But he also wanted a child.

And then Gigi came to the pivotal entry—the one that described the situation that would bring Arianna into their lives.

A daughter. It's finally happened. I'm going to be a mother. I know nothing about being a mother. I should be frightened beyond belief but somehow I just know that she's going to make our lives complete. And I have Gigi to help us. Thank God for Gigi. I think she's just as excited as I am, getting the nursery prepared and buying all the new bottles and things the baby will need.

Gigi couldn't help but smile when she read this entry.

She could remember that time vividly as probably the closest she'd felt with her employer. There had been a joy and openness to Mrs. Sinclair unlike anything Gigi had seen over the years since she'd begun working for them.

The truth was, Gigi had been thinking about leaving her job just prior to the announcement of the baby. But maybe a baby really would make things better, and it was clear to Gigi that Mrs. Sinclair was going to need a lot of help. Gigi had always been ready for a challenge—especially back then.

Everything changed for Gigi the day that the Sinclairs brought Arianna home from the hospital. She immediately fell in love with the beautiful dark-haired baby girl. Even though they'd hired a baby nurse for those first few infant months, it was Gigi who filled in the gaps with feedings and rocking the child to sleep—it was Gigi who seemed to bond with her, more so than Mrs. Sinclair, who always seemed to keep a slight distance—at least emotionally.

So much fell into place for her after reading the journal entries. Gigi had always felt a bit confused about the role she'd played in Arianna's life as a baby—and also anger toward Mrs. Sinclair, not understanding why she'd seemed to adopt a child that she really didn't want to make time for, or more importantly, to connect with.

At first, Gigi tried very hard not to overstep boundaries—but when it became clear that the infant and mother weren't really bonding, she couldn't not step in.

The child deserved to feel all the love in the world, and she'd get it from Gigi if not her own mother.

So, it was Gigi that fought for the role of nanny when it was time for the baby nurse to leave. Other housekeepers were brought in to be managed by her so that she could focus on looking after Arianna, and the rest—as they say—was history.

Gigi felt stunned as the reality of everything she'd read sunk in. A part of her had instantly connected to the fears and heartache that Mrs. Sinclair had written about. As a woman, she could relate very deeply to the emotion that had been poured out on those pages, and it caused her to have an exponential amount of compassion for a woman she'd once thought to be cold and even somewhat heartless. It wasn't a lack of love that had created distance between Mrs. Sinclair and Arianna. It had been the fear—and probably her own unforgiveness—that had kept her from real acceptance and love of her daughter.

Because of the letter Arianna had also found from her mother all those years ago, this wasn't a totally new idea to Gigi. She knew that Mrs. Sinclair had had regrets and that she did love Arianna—that much has been known before. But knowing this piece about what Mrs. Sinclair had been through before Arianna's birth—it caused Gigi to reexamine everything she thought to be true about the woman.

"Honey?"

Gigi didn't bother trying to hold her tears back as Douglas made his way to her.

CHAPTER 23

Gigi watched Douglas as he read the words for the first time, her arm around him as his body tensed.

Her husband had been friends with Mr. Sinclair since way before Gigi had been hired by them. It was quite possible that Douglas had actually known about the pregnancy—about the rape—but knowing her husband and his relationship with the Sinclairs, she guessed that this would be as big a shock for him as it had been for her.

He finished reading the second journal entry and reached for Gigi's hand. "Wow. I don't know exactly what to say—how to feel about this."

She could hear it in his voice—how much he was bothered by it all.

"So you had no idea?"

"None. I'm actually having a hard time believing it."

"But it must be true, right? I mean, it's not like she meant for anyone to ever find this."

Douglas shook his head. "I know. You're right. I just—that's not the guy I knew. Well, what do I know about how he must have felt? I mean, it couldn't have been easy for him, right?"

"Yes, but imagine how it had been for her."

"Oh, I know." Douglas leaned over to kiss her lightly on the cheek. "You're right. I'm not saying that anything about the situation was alright or justified or whatever." He sighed.

Gigi looked at him for a few minutes before she spoke the question that was on her mind.

"What is it?"

"Do you have any idea who it might have been? The man?"

Douglas shook his head. "No, I have no idea. I can't imagine who it could have been."

"For me, reading this sheds a lot of light on Mrs. Sinclair—why she acted the way she did most of the time. I always thought she was so cold, and it did used to upset me—when it came to Arianna. But I don't know, it's like these words she's written—it makes me judge her a lot less harshly, you know?"

"Yes, me too—what she must have been going through during that time."

"I always thought she was afraid of something and I could never understand where that came from. To me, it seemed like she had everything. Now I think that it was really her judging herself harshly. Maybe she just felt so undeserving of a child—of Arianna."

Douglas squeezed her hand.

"Anyway, there's more." Gigi gestured toward the book still in Douglas's lap.

Douglas opened the page to continue where he'd left off and as he reached the last entry, Gigi laid her head back against his chest so that she could also read the words.

Today was an impossible day. Arianna needed me—she wanted me so badly after school and I just couldn't handle it. She has so much energy and so much love. It's hard for me to be around her sometimes—to imagine that she wouldn't be better off with someone else as her mother. Thank God for Gigi. I don't know what I'd do without her. With her in Arianna's life, I can imagine that my daughter's going to turn out okay—that I won't be able to cause her too much damage. We really need to do something for Gigi—I need for her to know how much I appreciate her sticking by us all these years…I'll have to talk to him about that. I should be talking to my husband about a lot of things, I suppose. But at least I'm writing down my feelings again—and talking to my therapist. Perhaps some day, I'll be fixed enough to enjoy this life I have…

And that was the end of the journal—her final entry.

Douglas closed the book and placed his hands on Gigi's as she lay against his chest.

"It's a lot, right? To take in," said Gigi.

"It is. How are you feeling about it? I have to ask—did they do something for you? Something you can remember?"

When Gigi had read the words herself, she'd known exactly the time period that Mrs. Sinclair was referring to.

Arianna had been about six or seven and just starting to get very busy with homework and after-school activities. It was Gigi who had been there for all of it and by this time, it was her role—and not one that she'd ever complained about. Mrs. Sinclair was Mrs. Sinclair. Gigi had learned to not expect anything more from her, and she'd always just tried her best to make things okay for Arianna—to make things normal for the child.

Gigi squeezed Douglas's hand. "Yes, I'm pretty sure that it was around the time of this journal entry that they gave me a bonus followed by a huge raise. I remember feeling like it was a little out of the blue at the time and honestly, they never really said much at all about it. But I do feel like there was a point in time where things got really easy between us—Mrs. Sinclair and me. She would basically just let me do my own thing when it came to Arianna, sometimes joining us for certain things, but often not. It was just how it was."

"I'm glad to hear that. I bet it made them feel better too—about how things were."

"Does it all seem odd to you? Knowing Mr. Sinclair as well as you did?"

Douglas took a few seconds to respond. "It does, yes. If I'm being honest, it makes me question how well I really did know him. I do think he loved his family very much. I mean, I would never have wanted Arianna to question that."

"True. I don't think that she did. Not really. Well, I

know the letter she found from her mom went a long way in her understanding of Mrs. Sinclair. I'm really thankful that Ari had that before she died."

"Me too. She needed that—while she was trying to reconcile everything within herself."

"Honey?"

"Yes, love?"

"How much do you think we should share with the others about all this?"

Douglas was quiet again. "I think we can share everything with them. They're our family, and though this discovery is a sad reality, it involves Arianna, which I think means that they have a right to know—that they'd want to know."

"Good. I feel the same way. We'll tell them, then."

Gigi let herself relax in Douglas's arms, already feeling better for having shared the shocking discovery with him.

PAULA KAY

CHAPTER 24

Isabella reached over to hold Lia's hand after Gigi and Douglas had shared the contents of the journal with them. There was a heavy silence, and Isabella sensed Lia's tears before she saw them. She felt like crying herself—because what Mrs. Sinclair had been through had been so incredibly sad, but also—and maybe especially—because of the fracture it had caused in Arianna's relationship with her adoptive mother. Isabella guessed that Lia's tears were for Arianna as well.

"Are you okay?" said Blu to Lia.

Lia shook her head and looked like she was trying to pull herself together. "I will be. I think I'm just in shock. I knew that Arianna didn't have the best relationship with them—with Mrs. Sinclair—but I guess I'd made peace with it the same way that Arianna had seemed to. Well, it was Ari who'd convinced me that she'd made peace with it. It just makes me sad. Here I thought I was doing right by Arianna—that I never could have parented her the way she deserved, but—"

"—There were good times too, Lia." Gigi took Lia's hand in her own as she sat down next to her on the sofa.

"Please don't feel that you need to go back and relive your decisions."

"Yeah, that's the last thing Ari would have wanted," said Blu. "And you know that she was okay—in the end. She'd made peace with everything and I know that she wanted that for you too. It's interesting. It makes me have more sympathy for her—for Mrs. Sinclair—something I never actually thought I'd say."

"I feel the same," said Lucas. "I always tried so hard with them—to make them like me—but there was always a wall that I couldn't seem to get through."

"And as fathers, we know what it's like to want to protect our daughters," said Richard, his hand on Isabella's shoulder.

Isabella turned around to where Emily and Richard stood behind her. It was such an odd thing—and beautiful in a way—to think about the women in her life. They'd been through so much, each of their lives so different, yet connected by the common thread of motherhood, one that Isabella could now understand more completely than she ever had before.

She'd always thought of Emily—the mother who'd raised her—and Mrs. Sinclair as being so different. Though she wouldn't have said it out loud to anyone in so many words, she'd wondered how she'd gotten so much luckier than her birth mother when it came to the close relationship that she had with Emily. Isabella knew that it wasn't blood that defined the mother-child relationship, and she too felt more sympathy for Arianna's adoptive mother, after knowing some of what she'd been through herself.

Throughout the years, Isabella had learned to accept everything about her birth mother. Mostly she'd gotten positive information and occasionally she learned something about Arianna's life that really stretched her emotionally. But if there was one thing Isabella had learned, it was about embracing the future and the family that she now had—stronger than anything she ever could have imagined on that day when she'd first learned that her birth mother had passed away.

She felt Thomas's arm come around her, and she leaned in to kiss her sweet boy that he held in her arms. She watched across the yard as their daughter laughed and played with the children that were family to her. All around her, they were surrounded by family—by love—and Isabella knew that she could never want more than that. She'd been incredibly lucky in that regard.

PAULA KAY

CHAPTER 25

Blu took a sip of the hot chocolate that Chase handed her, and they stood hand in hand watching the kids run along the water's edge. She knew the water would be freezing, but the boys especially had begged to be able to at least put their feet in.

Chase brought her in close for a hug and nestled his lips to her forehead. "It's been a good day, hasn't it?"

Blu nodded. After the heaviness of the day before, a day out had been just what they'd all needed.

"I'm not at all sure that our gang is ready to leave tomorrow." She laughed.

The boys were chasing the twins, and Arianna and even Kylie and Gabriela had joined in on the fun. There was nothing Blu loved more than to see them all together with not a care in the world.

"No, I suppose they wouldn't mind staying longer," said Chase.

She felt his breath on her neck as he spoke.

"And you, my darling?"

"Well, I have no complaints about going home either—now that we're actually seeing one another every day," said Blu.

"Best decision we ever made, right?"

Blu nodded. Yes, they'd made the decision to slow down with their schedules at just the right time as far as she was concerned. She turned to kiss him on the cheek. "Yes, it was. And I'm very proud of you—of both of us, really—for being able to put work aside."

"Speaking of putting work aside…" Chase grinned at her.

"Yes? Go on."

"Well, I've had a bit of a brainstorm just today, actually."

"Do tell."

"I was thinking that it might be fun to spend the summer in San Diego. We could see if Jemma and the kids want to come. I think they'd really love the beach, and we've hardly spent any time at the beach house in years—other than your quick trips for work, I mean."

Blu let the idea sink in. Why hadn't they spent more time in La Jolla? They had a couple living in the house that took care of all the maintenance. She knew they'd be delighted to actually have a reason to get everything ready for them.

Jemma and Isabella walked over to them.

"You two look so deep in thought. Don't let us disturb you," said Jemma, laughing as Arianna ran to hide behind Isabella's legs.

"She sure does love being chased by those boys,

doesn't she?" said Blu.

Isabella laughed too as Arianna ran away from her now, Nicolas and Mateo close behind, letting her get just far enough ahead of them to be just out of reach. "She does, and that child sure does love the water. Look at her! I'd be worried if Thomas wasn't down there, although maybe I should go take Sammy from him."

Isabella turned to walk back toward the water and Blu put her arm around Jemma.

"You know, Chase and I were just talking…what would you think if we decided to spend the summer at the beach house? Would you guys be up for joining us?"

"Seriously? We'd love that! Well, of course I need to check with Rafael, but we've actually talked about it before, and the boys have been so excited about playing at the beach. That could be really fun. And we've not done that for ages, have we?"

"No, and never with all of us. We'll invite everyone. There's room." Blu looked at Chase, who was grinning at her.

"I guess that's a yes then?"

"I think that's a safe assumption. Let's plan for it!"

"Okay, now race you to the water!" Chase took off running, and Blu and Jemma just looked at one another and laughed.

"I'll go in a few minutes."

Jemma nodded. "It will be nice to have another big trip to look forward to. The boys are going to be over the moon."

"They sure do look happy. Chase and I were just talking about it—what a good time the kids seem to be having. They're growing so fast." Blu watched Jemma as she looked to where the kids were still laughing by the water. "You're a great mom, Jemma."

"Aww, thanks." Jemma leaned over to give her a big hug. "Well, I sure did have the best role model, didn't I?"

"Oh, I don't know about that, but somehow everything's worked out, hasn't it?"

Jemma grinned. "Yes. I'd say everything's worked out just fine."

CHAPTER 26

Gigi sipped her tea, enjoying the late afternoon breeze. There'd been a time—not so long ago—when even though it was enjoyable, she'd find herself flooded with memories whenever she'd sit outside in the garden. It had always taken some strength for her to overcome that feeling, pushing it aside to accept the gift that Arianna had left her.

Arianna—that sweet girl—had willed the house to Gigi for a reason, and Gigi had felt confident that she'd understood that reason. But finding Mrs. Sinclair's journal seemed to add another layer to everything Gigi had once believed about that time in her life.

She heard the door behind her, and moments later Douglas leaned down to kiss her before sitting on the small bench beside her.

"It's so quiet. They must be having a good time."

The whole gang minus Gigi and Douglas had decided to go into the city for one last day of sightseeing. Gigi had opted out, wanting a quiet last day after all the busyness of the week.

"Yes. Blu just texted me to say that they'd be heading back in about an hour—with some take-out for dinner." She reached over to hold Douglas's hand. "It's kinda nice having a little time for just us."

Douglas brought her hand to his lips. "I agree. I like it out here—a lot. They've done a good job keeping up the garden, haven't they?"

Gigi nodded.

"Honey, how are you feeling? You seem pretty quiet today."

Gigi smiled. "Oh, I'm okay. I suppose it's a little bittersweet—getting ready to leave tomorrow."

"I know what you mean—and finding the journal—well, that was really something, wasn't it?"

Gigi laughed lightly. "That's one way to put it. It definitely had my emotions in a bit of an unexpected state." She looked over at her husband. "It wasn't all bad, though—what we read in the journal. I have to say that reading Mrs. Sinclair's words about how she felt about me—well, it did make me feel good—and especially about being here. Maybe it's silly, but I can't help feeling that she'd kinda like knowing that so many good things had happened in this house of theirs."

"I think so."

Gigi could feel Douglas watching her.

"What? What are you not saying?"

"I often thought that maybe you felt that you didn't belong here—when we lived here before."

Gigi let his words sink in before answering him. It was true. She'd made the decision to sell very soon after they'd chosen to stay in Guatemala. The truth was that it had felt very odd to be in the house without Arianna there. And it was hard to imagine the house ever feeling like it belonged to them.

Gigi squeezed his hand. "I think you're right. I think maybe I never truly felt at home here, which is an odd thing to say because I lived here so many years before Arianna gave me the house. It's hard to explain really, but it just didn't feel right at the time."

"And now?"

"Now? I love being here. It's been a wonderful week. And yes, I do think that reading the words that Mrs. Sinclair wrote has cause me to feel differently being here. I guess it's almost as if I feel like I have her blessing or something. Is that crazy?"

"No, I don't think so." Douglas took a sip of his tea, while looking at her intently. "Honey?"

Gigi laughed. "Yes, dear."

"What would you say if I told you that George and Vivian want to sell the house?"

Gigi felt her heartbeat quicken. "Really?"

Douglas nodded.

"And you're thinking…"

"Well, to be honest, I hadn't really considered it seriously, but that was before our week here—and before finding the journal. And I know that Tuscany is our home now—and I don't think we'd want that to change, would we?"

Gigi was thinking—and feeling—trying to trust what her gut was telling her. Her home was definitely in Italy now but maybe…

She shook her head. "No, I don't think I'd want to move for good or anything, but—honey, if you're thinking about it as a vacation home? Maybe it's not such a bad idea?" She grinned. "In fact, I might just think that's one of the best ideas you've had in a long time."

Douglas grinned at her. "I think we could lock it down in a matter of weeks—if you want to? Maybe we'll go home and then come back in a couple months? Well, we can see how we feel, but I think we'd definitely come in the summer, don't you? And I'm sure the kids would love to come—"

"Am I included? And come where?" said Blu, laughing as she came outside followed by the twins, Arianna, Nicolas, and Mateo.

Gigi and Douglas looked at one another and laughed.

"Let's get everyone together," said Douglas.

Gigi turned toward the kids. "Chloe, Daisy, will you please ask everyone to come out?"

CHAPTER 27

Lia grinned as everyone gathered outside to hear what Gigi and Douglas had to say. There was always something happening in their family—usually some cause for celebration—and she welcomed it.

She felt Antonio's arm come around her waist and she turned slightly to kiss his cheek. "How are you doing? Feeling anxious to get back?"

"I had a quick conference call with the guys earlier and you know what? I think they've got a good handle on everything." He smiled.

"Well, miracle of all miracles, you actually look pretty relaxed telling me that." Lia teased him.

"And I feel pretty relaxed." He kissed her neck, sending shivers down her back. "Maybe next we should plan that trip to Paris you've been talking about?"

Lia laughed. "Well, that's a wonderful offer. I'm quite sure I'll take you up on that—once we're home and settled for a few weeks."

"Well, everyone, I guess we've got a little announcement to make." Gigi stood in front of them grinning as she looked at Douglas.

"Ooh, do tell. You know how much we like surprises," said Jemma.

"As it turns out, our friends that own this house are getting ready to put it on the market."

Lia saw Gigi squeeze Douglas's hand and she could sense her friend's excitement as she spoke.

"Is there an 'and' there?" Blu laughed.

"And we've decided that it would be a great idea to make this home ours again. We think it belongs in the family and we're hoping that you all will think it's as great an idea as we do—that you'd come back and use the house too."

"But I don't want you to move away." Arianna ran over to hug Gigi around the legs and Douglas scooped her up into his arms.

"We're not going to move away, sweetie. We'll just come here for vacations and we're hoping that you and Sammy will come join us sometimes. Would you like that?"

Arianna looked at Isabella. "Can we, Mommy?"

"Well, it sure sounds like a fun idea to me," said Isabella.

"I think it's fantastic! Do you guys have any idea of the timing?" asked Lia.

"I think we'll close pretty fast—within the month. I need to call them, but we're thinking Gigi will go back as planned and I'll come after I finalize everything here," said Douglas.

"And then we'd come back during the summer," said Gigi. "Maybe just for a few weeks to start, depending on what you all are doing."

"Well, actually…"

Lia saw the look that passed between Blu and Chase as Blu spoke.

"More news?" Isabella laughed as she shifted Samuel in her arms.

"Chase and I were talking earlier today about spending the summer at the beach house—and of course everyone's invited. With this news, maybe we can having a housewarming party here with Gigi and Douglas and split our time between the two places. What do you all think?"

"That sounds pretty perfect to me," said Gigi. "It feels like ages since I've been to the beach house."

"Ooh, me too," said Lia. She'd only been to Blu and Chase's home in La Jolla a few times and never for more than a couple days. The idea of enjoying that ocean view for a stretch of time was an invitation she'd not pass up—as long as Antonio felt alright about taking the time away. She looked over at him and as if reading her mind, he spoke.

"Lia and I were just talking about how surprisingly relaxed I'm feeling about being away from the vineyard. I think some summer travel plans for us sounds like a great idea."

"Well, it sounds like we're in for a great summer then," said Gigi and everyone nodded in agreement.

CHAPTER 28

Jemma had to stop herself from telling the kids to be careful for what felt like the hundredth time that morning. She and Rafael had brought the children to the park in the hopes of getting them good and tired before their long plane ride later that afternoon.

"Honey, they're going too high. Don't you think?"

She'd had to learn to loosen up a lot since the boys had joined their family. It seemed, according to Rafael, that the girls were really mostly okay playing with their older brothers. It was Jemma's job, though, to determine where that "mostly okay" trod on being too dangerous for the younger girls.

She laughed at the look on Rafael's face.

"Well, they *are* going so high—much higher than they've ever gone before. I'm sure of that."

Rafael squeezed her hand before he let it go to walk closer to where the boys were pushing Chloe and Daisy on the swing set.

"Girls?"

"Yes, Daddy," said Chloe.

"Are you hanging on very tight?"

"We are!" screamed Daisy as the Nicolas pushed her even harder.

"Okay, good." Rafael turned his attention toward the boys. "I think that's high enough boys, okay?"

"Okay, Dad," said Mateo.

It was instant—the tears on Jemma's face as her husband turned around to come back toward her. She hugged him tight and when he whispered in her ear, asking if she'd heard what Mateo had called him, she couldn't speak for the lump in her throat.

She nodded her head and smiled as her husband quickly brushed his hand across the wetness on his own cheeks, looking intently at her as he took her hand in his once again.

"He said it so easily," said Jemma, watching the kids as the warmth of loving them spread throughout her entire body. "Isn't it odd? I mean, you hear others talk about it—about how much your heart can expand, but if I'm honest, Raf—I didn't know what it would be like. I didn't know that I could really fall in love with those two kids as easily as I have. I swear, I couldn't love them more if they had come from my own body, and it's astounding to me to even say that—so soon, I mean."

Again she felt her eyes welling with tears, and this time it was Rafael who reached out to wipe his finger under her eyes, before kissing her gently on the mouth.

"Do you have any idea—could you possibly know the

depth of love I have for you?"

Rafael's voice was husky and the look he gave her was one that made her wish that they were back in the privacy of their room. She kissed him back, more passionately than she'd intended, and it was Daisy's voice that brought her attention back to the world around her.

"K-I-S-S-I-N-G!"

Jemma laughed. "Who taught you that?"

"Mateo taught us the song—and Mommy, you and Daddy kiss a lot!"

Chloe was also at her side now with the boys coming up behind them.

Jemma laughed. "Well, honey, I hope that one day when you are *much* older, you will have a husband that you love to kiss as much as I love to kiss your daddy."

"Ewww. Never," said Chloe.

Rafael reached down to grab each of his girls—one in each arm.

"Well, for now, your Daddy's cheeks will get all of your kisses. Come on now." He grinned as the girls, now giggling, obediently covered his face with kisses.

Jemma knelt down, putting her arms around Nicolas and Mateo as she first kissed them on the cheek and then hugged them tight.

"I love my family." Nicolas's words were barely a whisper in Jemma's ear.

"Me too, honey," Jemma whispered into her youngest son's ear.

Rafael caught Jemma's eye as he put the girls back down on the grass.

"Group hug, everybody!"

Jemma laughed as Rafael's arm came first around her, and then together with her, they pulled the rest of the kids in close to them. She knew how lucky she was—to have won the heart of such a man. Rafael had somehow managed to make her every dream come true. She couldn't possibly think of what could make her feel any more complete than what she was feeling in that moment with her family.

CHAPTER 29

Blu grinned as Gigi placed the warm scone in front of her. The house was oddly quiet, and she welcomed the opportunity to spend a little time with Gigi on her own.

"Where is everyone?"

"Jemma and Rafael went to the park with the kids, Lia and Bella wanted to get in one last walk on the bridge, and all the others are either out to breakfast with Lucas and Kate or at the mall with your husband."

Blu nodded. "Oh, right. I overheard that conversation between Kylie and Chase this morning—some new shop that her friends had been telling her about. And you? Not in the mood to go out to breakfast this morning?"

Gigi smiled. "Nope. It seemed fitting to me to make one last batch of these and have my coffee here in the garden on our last day—it's all the more delightful that you are joining me, my dear."

"Thanks. I appreciate that and your scones very much." Blu looked at Gigi sitting across from her and then she reached across the table to take her hand. "Thank you for bringing us here. I just want you to know

159

that it means a lot to me. I've loved every minute of it."

"It has been wonderful. I loved having you here—it's especially comfortable with you, Blu. I want you to know that. I feel a certain peace with you here. You and I have the most memories in this house and—I don't know, it's almost as if I can sense Arianna's smile as we sit here now. Does that sound crazy?"

Blu shook her head. "Nope, not crazy. I know exactly what you mean. If I close my eyes to enjoy the smell of your scone and coffee along with the quietness of the garden, I swear that the next thing I hear could be Arianna's laugh as she comes through the door to join us. It's strange how it can feel as if no time has passed, yet the years have brought so many changes, haven't they? For all of us, I mean."

"Yes, they have. And I'm at a point where I'm ready for even more change, I think. There used to be a time in my life that it frightened me just a little. When things were good, I didn't want to rock the boat—for fear of it all vanishing, I suppose."

Blu squeezed her hand. "We've both learned a thing or two about trust, I'd say. And I think the good men in our lives have had a lot to do with that."

"Well, that's something I'd agree with." Gigi smiled at her. "Yes, I'd say that one thing about growing older is that you learn to roll with things a bit more. It's something I hope that I've learned by this point in my life, anyway."

"Well, I certainly think you have."

Douglas's voice behind them startled them both.

"Sorry, honey, I was just coming out to see if I could help with anything—would you like me to set the table for you?"

Gigi looked at her watch. "Yes, I suppose it is getting to be that time, isn't it? Lia's got everything prepped with instructions about what goes into the oven at what time, and they'll be back soon."

Blu stood up. "I'll help."

"Thanks, honey." Gigi got up too and the two women hugged. "I hope that you and I will have many more mornings together here like this."

"I'm betting that we will." Even as she spoke, Blu felt herself planting the memory of the moment in her mind—just in case. She'd learned to appreciate the moments in her life for what they were—and sometimes they were not as easily recreated.

PAULA KAY

CHAPTER 30

Isabella laughed as Lia handed her the stocking cap that she pulled out of her bag. They were about a quarter of the way across the bridge and the wind was already whipping her hair in every direction.

"You just happened to have an extra cap in your purse?"

Lia smiled. "No, I brought it for you."

"Well, thank you for thinking of me." Isabella grinned and reached for her grandmother's hand. "I always forget, even though I know it gets cold here."

The two walked in silence until they were about to the center of the bridge, a favorite stopping point for Isabella to look out across the bay toward the landscape of San Francisco.

"It's such a clear morning. I love the weather when it's like this," said Lia.

Isabella nodded and was quiet for a few seconds as she looked out across the water. She'd already had many discussions with Lia about the significance of this walk—of the bridge—when it came to the memories the others had of Arianna. Somehow just walking it herself brought her peace and a feeling of connection with her birth mother.

"Me too," she said. "Shall we turn around?"

Lia looked at the time on her phone. "Yes, I suppose so. I left instructions with Gigi about getting lunch started but I hate for her to do it. She was so insistent that we go this morning, though. I kinda got the feeling that maybe she wanted a little quiet time at the house as well."

"It has been busy, that's for sure. But in a good way, right? And the kids have been great."

"The kids have been great. I don't think any of that bothers anyone, least of all Gigi and Douglas. You know how much she loves having the kids around."

Isabella leaned over to give Lia a big hug. "Thanks for coming here with me this morning. It felt like the right thing to do before we leave today—in honor of my mother, I suppose."

Lia kissed her on the cheek. "Your mother would have been so proud of you, Bella—of the woman you've become—the mother you are to your kids. I hope that knowing that brings you a feeling of peace."

Isabella nodded as she linked her arm in Lia's and they started to make their way back to the parking lot. Being back in Marin had only ever given Isabella an overwhelming sense of peace and more of an understanding of who her mother had been—something that Isabella would always welcome.

CHAPTER 31

Gigi smiled as she looked around the table. The backdrop might keep changing, but so many of her best memories were of the entire family sharing a meal together. And this last meal before they all headed home felt even more special for some reason.

Perhaps it was the memory of Arianna so vivid outside in the garden, or the fact that being with Douglas, Blu, and Lia there felt like the most natural thing in the world, as if time had stood still for them—enough so, anyway, that they might enjoy the rush of all the good memories that they each shared in this space.

She looked toward the smaller table set up near the swing set. The kids' table was growing year after year, evidence of their expanding family; and if Gigi had to guess, she'd think that there might be more kids in the future for Isabella and Thomas, such wonderful parents and so proud of the children they were raising.

It was funny to Gigi that even though she wasn't blood related to any of them, she felt such a strong connection—a bond that had never been questioned and one that she didn't imagine ever could be broken.

She laughed as Antonio pulled a reluctant Lia down into her chair at the table—Lia ever the hostess and every dish impeccably delicious, regardless of where they were or the ingredients she managed to locate at the local market.

Gigi thought it had been the best birthday she'd ever celebrated, one that would hold its place in her memory for years to come.

As if reading her mind, Douglas stood to give the toast, reaching for her hand to pull her up beside him.

"Gigi and I want to thank you all for coming—for making her birthday special and for being such a big part of our lives."

She smiled at them all, her heart full, her eyes wet with tears of happiness as she spoke. "We love you all and will look forward to creating many more memories here with you." She leaned over to kiss Douglas before continuing. "And here's to the exciting unknown—where good things happen as long as we're all together."

As glasses clinked and shouts of "Cheers" rang out around the table, Gigi froze the memory in her mind. Yes, she knew that with the love and support of this crazy, wonderful family around her, she could handle anything that came her way.

ABOUT THE AUTHOR

Paula Kay spent her childhood in a small town alongside the Mississippi River in Wisconsin. (Go Packers!) As a child, she used to climb the bluffs and stare out across the mighty river—dreaming of far away lands and adventures.

Today, by some great miracle (and a lot of determination) she is able to travel, write and live in multiple locations, always grateful for the opportunity to meet new people and experience new cultures.

She enjoys Christian music, long chats with friends, reading (and writing) books that make her cry and just a tad too much reality TV.

Paula loves to hear from her readers and can be contacted via her website where you can also download a complimentary book of short stories.

PaulaKayBooks.com

ALL TITLES BY PAULA KAY

http://Amazon.com/author/paulakay

The Complete Legacy Series:
Buying Time
In Her Own Time
Matter of Time
Taking Time
Just in Time
All in Good Time

A Map for Bella:
Bella's Hope
Bella's Holiday
Bella's Heart
Bella's Home

Legacy Series Reunion:
Christmas in Tuscany
Birthday Surprise
A Summer Together

Visit the author website at PaulaKayBooks.com to get
on the notification list for new releases, information
about new series and to also receive the complimentary
download of "The Bridge: A Collection of Short Stories."

Made in United States
North Haven, CT
21 September 2022

24395297R00093